ATTENTION & INTERPRETATION THERAPY (AIT):

A PERSONAL WORKBOOK

Adapted from: Train Your Brain.... Engage Your Heart.... Transform Your Life: A Course in Attention & Interpretation Therapy (AIT)

AMIT SOOD, MD MSc

Director of Research and Practice, Mayo CIM Program
Chair, Mayo Mind Body Initiative
Associate Professor of Medicine
Mayo Clinic Rochester, MN

Enhance present moment awareness;

Embody greater wisdom and love;

Nurture a healthier brain;

Be kind to the self; and

End suffering

By

Cultivating heartfulness

TABLE OF CONTENTS

Disclaimer

The information in this book is not intended to substitute a physician's advice or medical care. Please consult your physician or other health care provider if you are experiencing any symptoms or have questions pertaining to the information contained in this book.

The contents in this book represent the personal opinions of the author and are not endorsed by Mayo Clinic.

The Journey you are about to take

Attention and Interpretation Therapy: A Personal Workbook intends to walk with you on a journey. This journey will take you from the past and future to the present moment; from lesser to higher wisdom; from suffering to joy; from the ego to the self; and toward greater love. The journey *trains your brain's higher center* to help you decrease the negative ruminations of the mind and enhance its engagement with the present moment and its contents. The journey *engages your heart* to fill the present moment with greater love.

The four wheels of the journey are *neurosciences, psychology, philosophy, and spirituality*. The voyage entails the progressive unfolding of *wisdom and love*. In this journey you will pick six precious jewels: *enhanced present moment awareness, gratitude, compassion, acceptance, forgiveness, and higher meaning and purpose*. The path overcomes five impediments: *ignorance, cravings, aversions, excessive ego, and attention deficit*. In the process you will likely experience four key milestones: *peace, joy, resilience, and altruism*. Each of these milestone points toward one common destination—*transformation (awakening)*. The entire journey can be summarized in three words—*cultivating greater heartfulness*.

Increasing *peace,* contentment and equanimity take away much of anxiety, allow a better anchor in the present moment, and provide a deep sense of fulfillment and comfort. *Joy* is a welcome accompaniment of peace. This joy originates in freedom and is often not contingent on something extraordinary happening. A healthy meal, a casual hello, a kind email, watching children play, sun shining in the sky—any or all of these can be a source of intense joy. *Resilience* refers to your ability to not only withstand adversity but bounce ever so higher, sometimes because of adversity. Resilience emerges when you are grateful for your blessings, when you accept the present moment and its contents, when your compassion effortlessly flows toward self and others, when you cultivate greater forgiveness, and when you are anchored in a higher meaning and purpose of your life.

Peace, joy and resilience although hardwired within us, still remain hiding and have to be purposefully discovered. Discover how? In search of an answer, I am reminded of Michelangelo when he said, *"Every block of stone has a statue inside it and it is the task of the sculptor to discover it."* This process of discovery entails removing the extra rock and sand that hides the statue. That extra stuff within us likely is the excessive thoughts and feelings, the negative ruminations that originate in cravings and aversions. Imbalanced cravings and aversions in turn depend on egocentricity and ignorance that give rise to excessive self focus with resulting deficits in *altruism*.

It is the progressive cultivation of *altruism,* the fourth milestone on this journey that helps you discover peace, joy and resilience. Altruism recognizes the universality of suffering and finiteness, and is deeply anchored in interconnectedness. Altruism believes we all have an innate capacity to decrease our individual as well as collective suffering. Developing altruism and its practical application—daily kindness, is a choice waiting for you to exercise.

So to awaken the Michelangelo within, we need to cultivate a deeper and purer wisdom and love that leads us toward altruism, which in turn balances our cravings and aversions. Such wisdom and love flow from us when our brain is trained and heart engaged in enhanced present moment awareness embodying greater gratitude, compassion, acceptance, forgiveness, and higher meaning and purpose—*a state of heartfulness.* The extra stuff, those excessive thoughts and negative ruminations, automatically get shed in the process. Peace, joy, resilience and altruism emerge from their hiding, your brain rewires and the heart engages, as you walk on a path toward transformation (awakening).

Salmon swim upstream to spawn and thus secure the continuation of her species. We have to swim upstream to discover and unfold the highest being within us.

Introduction

This workbook provides you a personal program to understand and embody the concepts and skills related to Attention and Interpretation Therapy (AIT). AIT program has been developed to offer participants a scientific, structured, pragmatic and efficient approach to decrease stress and enhance resilience.

AIT addresses two aspects of human experience, attention and interpretation. Research studies suggest that the human mind instinctively and often excessively focuses on threats and imperfections. Since a considerable amount of imperfections exist within the domains of the past and the future, attention commonly gets mired in the psychological frame of time, disengaged from the present moment. This predisposes to excessive thinking, ineffective efforts toward thought suppression, and avoidant response. The process once initiated perpetuates itself because of the changes in the brain that incrementally predispose you to sustain the stress response and spend excessive amount of time with ruminations, worrying, planning and problem solving.

AIT will help train your attention and interpretations. Attention training will help to make your attention more focused, relaxed, altruistic, non-judgmental, in the present moment, sustained and purposeful. This will provide your attention a delightful alternative to the negative ruminations and worrying—the novelty of the world. Complementing attention training are instructions to help you direct your interpretations away from fixed prejudices toward a more flexible disposition. Prejudices are replaced by five core values: gratitude, compassion, acceptance, forgiveness, and higher meaning and purpose. Trained interpretations thus provide you a highly desirable alternative to the judgments and bias—the higher principles.

The program synthesizes wisdom from four key disciplines: *neurosciences, psychology, philosophy, and spirituality*. The primary skills you will learn are *enhanced present moment awareness, gratitude, compassion, acceptance, forgiveness, higher meaning and purpose, and a personal relaxation program*. These skills may help you enhance self regulation so you have better self control, particularly with respect to diet, exercise, and balancing work and play. The program will also train your executive functions so you have better attention, are more proactive, have better judgment and decision making ability, have greater ability to postpone gratifications, and are better able to handle complexity and novelty.

We teach the program individually or in groups in two basic formats: an abbreviated version called the Stress Management and Resiliency Training Program (SMART Program); and a longer version described as the full AIT course. The SMART program is generally taught over 60-90 minutes in group or individual sessions while the full AIT course is taught in group sessions over two days with the possibility of continuing the instructions via teleconference and other media as a follow up. The basis of the program, practice exercises and the entire structured approach is fully described in the book, *Train Your Brain…Engage Your Heart…Transform Your life*, from which this workbook is derived.

Section I: Basic Concepts

1. Do not postpone joy

Exercise 1. In which of the following aspects is your life presently challenged? Check all that apply.

1. Relationships ☐
2. Children ☐
3. Health ☐
4. Finances ☐
5. Work ☐
6. Personal ☐
7. Others ☐

Exercise 2. Do you think your challenges are likely to increase / decrease / go away / or remain the same over the ensuing years? Check the most likely option (Table 1.1).

	Increase	Decrease	Go away	Unchanged
Relationships	☐	☐	☐	☐
Children	☐	☐	☐	☐
Health	☐	☐	☐	☐
Finances	☐	☐	☐	☐
Work	☐	☐	☐	☐
Personal	☐	☐	☐	☐
Others:	☐	☐	☐	☐
	☐	☐	☐	☐

Table 1.1 Direction of future challenges

In most situations you may have noticed that the stressors will likely increase, decrease, or remain about the same. Most of our stressors tend not to go away.

An important pearl to learn from this exercise is – ***"Do not postpone joy"***

Do not postpone joy waiting for a day when life will be perfect and all your stressors will be gone. If you wait because you are too busy or stressed, it might be a wait of a lifetime.

Your opportunity to live the best you can is in this very moment. If you let go of this opportunity you might come back to it, may be a decade later. Precious time will be lost in the process.

You will always have some excuse to postpone your joy. I myself have never had a day when my boat was fully secure in the harbor, the water was a deep blue, the winds were quiet, and the sun was bright and shining in the sky. Waiting for such a day would be a very long wait. So I need to admit the reality and find fulfillment in the present moment accepting all its imperfections.

This is the day the LORD has made; let us rejoice and be glad in it (Psalm 118:24 NIV).

The important next question then is – what gets in the way of your joy?

2. Stress

Joy is often pushed away when you feel excessively stressed in your life. Stress is perceived when the demands placed on you exceed your capacity to meet those demands. Stress primarily results from an interaction between the actual events in your life and how you perceive them. The reality is that the actual events may or may not be amenable to change. **You, however, always have the option to influence your perception and response.**

Exercise 1. How do you usually perceive your stressors? Check all that apply.

1. Punishment ☐

2. Defeat ☐

3. Loss ☐

4. Enemy ☐

5. Challenge ☐

6. Value ☐

7. Opportunity ☐

8. Growth ☐

If you see your stressors as punishment / defeat / loss / or enemy, you are likely to add additional layers of emotional suffering. Such stressors may form the nidus for negative memories that lodge in your mind and may force you away from the wonders of your life. By appraising stressors as challenge / value / opportunity / or growth, you are more likely to learn from them and cope adaptively.

In actuality most of what stresses you can prompt you toward growth. See if any of the options below make sense to you.

Exercise 2. Can you find something positive about your present or previous stressor/s? Check all that apply.

1. Helped you come closer to a relative or friend ☐

2. Gave you an opportunity to learn ☐

3. Helped you develop a broader outlook toward life ☐

4. Provided you an impetus to connect with your spirituality ☐

5. Helped you cultivate greater appreciation for your blessings ☐

6. Instilled within you the feelings of gratitude for what you have ☐

7. Tested your resilience and thus made you stronger ☐

8. Other_____ ☐

Being able to find meaning and something positive amidst adversity is the hall-mark of resilience. Each year approximately 136 million new babies are born on our planet.   I am sure most moms do not recall the pain of childbirth as suffering. This is because there exists a precious positive meaning associated with this pain—the birth of a beautiful baby. The pain of a kidney stone however almost always brings suffering.

Greater stress is also felt when you perceive a lack of control. Patients who are em-powered to choose their treatment plan feel a better sense of control and are more likely to accept the treatment and its outcomes.

Thus stress comes from pain or adversity that is:

- *greater* **than an individual's capacity to handle it;**

- **does not have adequate** *meaning* **for it;**

- **is not within a person's** *control*; **and**

- **is not** *accepted.*

We may not have much control over the stressors. However, our perceptions greatly depend on us. And it is our perceptions that determine how we respond to disruptions.

3. Our response to disruptions

We all get disrupted at one time or the other. Disruptions push us toward a state of imbalance, at least for the short term. How we come out of the disruption depends on a number of variables, most importantly how we respond. A model developed by researchers that depicts the outcome of disruptions is shown below (Figure 3.1).

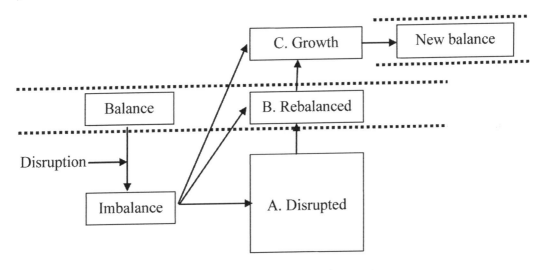

Figure 3.1 Our response to disruptions

The outcome of disruptions or imbalance, thus could be one of three:

A) Disrupted – Prolonged state of disruption;

B) Rebalanced – Achieving balance once again; or

C) Growth – Growth as a result of disruption.

Over a period of time, most people progress from the disrupted state to a state of growth. However, the progress tends to be slower than desirable.

Exercise: What would be your preferred response to a disruption?

1. Remain disrupted   ☐
2. Re-establish balance   ☐
3. Grow through disruption   ☐

Your ability to rapidly grow through disruption can be called your resilience. Resilience partly depends on how you perceive, appraise and respond to your stressor/s. If you perceive your stressors as punishment / defeat / loss / or enemy, you will more likely remain disrupted. On the other hand, if you appraise your stressors as challenge / value / opportunity / or growth, you will more likely grow through adversity. Resilience thus depends on your ability to find *meaning* in a stressor. Resilience also depends on your perception that you have some level of *control* over the outcomes.

In the foregoing, we have referred to perceptions several times. Let us do an exercise to really understand how our perceptions can sometimes make all the difference.

4. Is it a source of stress or joy?

Exercise: List everything in the world that makes you happy today.

1. _____ ☐

2. _____ ☐

3. _____ ☐

4. _____ ☐

5. _____ ☐

6. _____ ☐

7. _____ ☐

Now go back and check mark those that may be a source of stress in the past or present, or could be a future stressor.

Welcome to the world that is at the same time Joyville and Stressville! In every home of this village, every nook and corner, stress abounds. But so does opportunity and joy. The two are often inseparable; when you pick one you almost always pick the other. What would you rather do? Stay passive for the fear of displeasure or embrace all your opportunities? It might help to accept and in some instances even like all that challenges you. **The face might look like that of a stressor; the body, however, often is that of opportunity.**

Work, family, health, finances—all your challenges are also your playing ground, your life breath. How can you let them go? Life without these challenges might become boring and unproductive. Life is a beautiful mosaic with multiple colors. All these colors have their place. Absolute good is an imaginary entity. Everything in the world is a combination of good and bad—it is all contextual. See how each of the colors fit together; be an observer of apparent imperfections. Try to embrace the imperfections. This is the first and most essential step toward their transformation—toward your transformation.

Like an appetizing menu, many (but not all) things in life are here for the asking. Do not place your request based on what you see on others' tables. Create your own plate based on your preferences, appetite, and palate. Make sure you keep enough servings of love and peace, not just as a dessert at the end of the dinner, but also as a part of the main course.

We have seen so far that the way you perceive and respond to your stressors has a profound impact on the outcome of disruptions in your life. These perceptions to a great extent depend on the contents of your mind.

5. Contents of the mind

Your response to a stressor depends on the contents of your mind—your thoughts and related emotions. If you were to assess your thoughts on two basic parameters, quality and number, the table below illustrates the four possibilities (Table 5.1).

Quality of thinking ⟶	Negative thoughts	Positive thoughts
⬇ Number of thoughts		
Few	Depressed Apathetic A	Attentive Mindful/Heartful B
Many	Anxious Angry C	Excited Energized D

Table 5.1 Quality of thinking, number of thoughts and your daily experience

It might help to self assess your overall disposition through the day by answering the question that follows.

Exercise: What percentage of your day is spent in modes represented by the four boxes?

A – Few mostly negative thoughts   _____%

B – Few mostly positive thoughts   _____%

C – Many mostly negative thoughts _____%

D – Many mostly positive thoughts   _____%

In general, when you are anxious or angry (quadrant C) you have excessive thoughts that are often negative (the words "negative thoughts" connote thoughts that have the flavor of insecurity, bias, predominant self-focus, and excessive use of prejudices). You also have excessive thoughts when you are excited, energized, and animated (quadrant D). These states are usually in response to receiving unexpected positive energy from the world in some form. The excited state, however, is energy intensive and not sustainable over the long haul. The excited state often ends in a depressed, anxious, or even angry state if the expectations are not fully met by reality. It would be optimal to move toward quadrant B by cultivating a mind with optimal number of positive thoughts.

There are two important steps toward that goal – 1) Training your attention; and 2) Refining your interpretations. These two steps together constitute the Attention and Interpretation therapy (AIT). **In combination these steps take you toward enhanced present moment awareness that is embodied with greater gratitude, compassion, acceptance, meaning & purpose, and forgiveness—a state of *heartfulness*.**

6. Heartfulness

I like to define heartfulness as, *"Practicing presence with love."* A more elaborate definition is, *"Enhancing awareness of the present moment and its contents and embodying the present moment with greater gratitude, compassion, acceptance, forgiveness, and higher meaning and purpose."*

Heartfulness emphasizes filling the mind with more of heart, i.e. love; Hence the *focus on engaging the heart (or the heartful part of the brain). Heartfulness intends to make the brain more heartful.* Such brain and mind are resilient and can better resist the weeds of negative thoughts from growing.

In many languages, mind and heart have the same word *"dil."* Heartfulness, thus includes a combination of the core process of the human mind i.e. attention and the core process of the human heart i.e. interpretation with love. **Heartfulness has two main anchors—wisdom and love.**

Among the many components of wisdom that contribute to heartfulness are recognizing and accepting the reality of suffering, finiteness, and change. Heartfulness compassionately recognizes the proclivity of the human mind to dwell excessively in the psychological time of the past and future. The vast proportion of human suffering being in these two time zones, heartfulness gently guides the human mind toward finding greater value within the present moment.

Human mind, however, may have spent a lifetime escaping from the present moment. Heartfulness, thus does not "stress" the human mind by leaving it without anchors in the vast expanse of the present moment, a territory that may seem initially unfamiliar. Heartfulness offers two anchors—externally the novelty of the world and internally the feeling of love in the form of gratitude, compassion, acceptance, forgiveness, and meaning and purpose. With practice, it is possible for the mind to attain a state of abiding peace and may transcend the needs for any anchor. Heartfulness allows this process to unfold at its own pace, not necessarily setting this as a goal but only a milestone in a long journey.

Heartfulness is cheerfulness. Cultivating heartfulness allows you to carry a little heaven with you wherever you go. It allows you to nurture a cheerful heart (and brain).

A cheerful heart has a continual feast (Proverbs 15:15).

Heartfulness is not preconceptual, prelogical or prior to duality. Heartfulness does not deny the existence or non-existence of thoughts, but focuses on softening the relationship with the thoughts.

The purpose of heartfulness is to guide the aspirant to a state of lasting peace and joy. Peace and joy are emergent properties and cannot be forcefully willed. Dance of the peacocks, natural mirthful giggle of children at play, state of flow in your work, or an experience of deep meditation; these are all emergent properties. They cannot be artificially created. They flow out spontaneously from the depth of the heart. An essential ingredient required for peace and joy to emerge within human awareness, an ingredient that is a synthesis of wisdom and love and a core concept of heartfulness is *altruism.*

Altruism, described as a concern for the welfare of others often with selfless intention, provides the path toward heartfulness. Altruism recognizes the universality of suffering and finiteness. Importantly, altruism is deeply anchored in interconnectedness. Thus altruism recognizes that suffering is a common human experience, and by virtue of us being interconnected, we are affected by the suffering of the others, and importantly, have within our capacity to decrease suffering. Developing altruism and its practical application—daily kindness, is a choice we all have.

We all have the choice to embody the five essential values to develop altruism (and thus peace and joy). The five values are that of gratitude, compassion, acceptance, forgiveness, and meaning and purpose. A combination of these values adds up to the universal treasure of love that is at the core of heartfulness. These skills and the reflections drawn from them provide an immediately available alternative to negative ruminations. We thus do not just empty the present moment, we fill it with love. Peace, joy and resilience are a natural outcome of exercising the choice to cultivate altruism and daily kindness. It is this kindness that we should wear daily as a jewel on us. Everything that is good naturally follows.

Don't ever forget kindness and truth. Wear them like a necklace. Write them on your heart as if on a tablet. (Proverb 3:3 NCV)

Heartfulness and Mindfulness:

You might be asking, what is the difference between heartfulness and mindfulness, if any?

Both heartfulness and mindfulness are slightly different flavors of looking at the same state of the mind. Mindfulness, as commonly understood focuses on purposeful present moment awareness in a non-judgmental fashion. Like mindfulness, heartfulness also emphasizes on enhancing engagement with the present moment but has a more *explicit* focus on experiencing the present moment with greater love. Further, the present moment in heartfulness is flexible (from just this moment to an entire lifetime) depending on the individual situation and load. In a high load situation in the midst of disruption, the present moment may be shrunk to just this second and one might live one's life one second at a time and carry only the load of this moment. On the contrary when the circumstances are more favorable, the present moment can be expanded. Thus heartfulness emphasizes flexibility along with balance.

In essence, however, any difference that is perceived is only superficial. **Understood deeply, mindfulness includes heartfulness and heartfulness includes mindfulness.** Both emphasize that the present moment is not a means to an end—it is the end in itself. Heartfulness and mindfulness both create egoless and non-reactive awareness, a pure state of being. They are a bit like wisdom and love. **At a deeper level, wisdom includes love and love includes wisdom.** They both overlap, almost completely. So does mindfulness and heartfulness.

I include both the constructs with the primary intention of emphasizing to you and leaving no doubt in your mind that we are not simply attempting to empty the mind, we are focusing on enhancing presence of love with its five attributes of gratitude, compassion, acceptance, forgiveness, and meaning and purpose.

A constant practice of *"presence with love"* may take us to a state of *"prayer without ceasing."* Life, work, relationships all become a prayer. It is to such a state we wish to travel. It is a very worthy journey the important milestones on which are peace, joy, resilience, and altruism.

One of the most important tools you use to move toward peace, joy, resilience and altruism is your brain. Let me introduce you to your brain, its two centers and two networks.

7. Your Brain, its two centers and two networks

The brain is an unimaginably complex organ. It has over 100 billion neurons with almost infinite connections between them.

The two centers

A useful oversimplification for the present purpose will be to focus on the two centers of the brain that are of central importance to your well-being—the higher (cortical) and the lower (limbic) centers. *Increased activity of the lower limbic center makes you anxious, unhappy, depressed, and stressed. Activation of the brain's higher cortical center helps you be calm, happy, joyous, and resilient.* The relationship is almost mathematical. The main constituent of the lower limbic center is the amygdala, while the most significant component of the higher cortical center is the pre-frontal cortex. *The beauty is that you have a great deal of choice to activate one or the other brain center. Look at these centers as tools available to you to run your life.*

The higher cortical center helps you with many essential functions including, attention, judgment, decision making, memory, focus, postponing gratification, abstract thinking, compassion, forgiveness, handling complexity and novelty, and many more. With the present world being so fast paced and complex, this part of the brain, although much larger in us than any other species, has to be engaged and activated fully to support our pattern of living.

Instinctively, however, many of us have a low threshold to activate the lower limbic center, particularly if we have an overactive mind. It is almost as if the connection to the limbic center is by a short, fast, broad band while that to the cortical center is by a long, slow, narrow band (Figure 7.1). Evolutionarily this pattern of connection helped us survive as a species. If you are born with a propensity to feel depressed, anxious, or stressed, you likely have a particularly active limbic system.

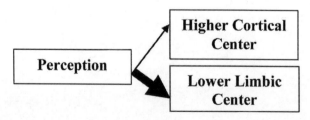

Figure 7.1 The "broad band" connection to the lower limbic center;
"narrow band" connection to the higher cortical center

A good rule of thumb about the brain can be stated thus: if you engage a part of the brain, you awaken and empower it. Thus the limbic system (comprised mainly of the amygdala), once activated, makes its own connections stronger. *A key aspect of this whole process is that <u>the chemicals (stress mediators) released in the stress response not only strengthen the limbic system but also disempower the higher cortical system</u>. Let me repeat it, <u>the chemicals (stress mediators) released in the stress response not only strengthen the limbic system but also disempower the higher cortical system</u>.*

This may keep you within the trap of an activated limbic system for much longer than optimal (Figure 7.2). Stress and depression, thus cause damage to your brain. No wonder scientists have begun to call the effect of stress on the brain as a reversible neurodegenerative disorder.

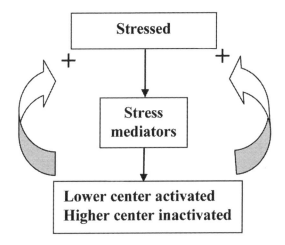

Figure 7.2 Feedback loops between stress, stress mediators, and the brain centers

Do you see the elaborate set up—how the inefficient systems in your brain can fence you into suffering and then enslave you into that state? This is like a boa constrictor—stress begets more stress because of this imperfection in our biology. The process is more common than you may think. In fact, this faulty mechanism is ubiquitous and to my mind, a very important contributor to the collective suffering on our planet.

The reason our brain responds this way is because we have learned over the years to strengthen the part of the brain that we are more likely to use. Limbic center is very useful for short-term acute stressors. Hence, we strengthen it when stressed. However, in modern times, most of our stressors tend to be chronic, which our brain is not very well trained to respond to. It is for this reason that the brain's instinctive efforts to help us often become maladaptive.

The two networks

The latest research in neurosciences suggests that the complex brain circuitry can be divided into two broad networks.

1. Task positive network – this is the *externally focused network* that helps you perceive and interact with the world. Think about a time when you were deeply absorbed in doing something that you really enjoyed. Hours may have passed by but only felt like a few minutes. The experience was rejuvenating and did not produce any fatigue. In this activity, often described as a state of "flow," you might have forgotten yourself for a moment, and did not experience any mind wandering. In this state you experienced the perfect activation of task positive network.

2. Default network – the network of neurons that host the default network are involved in *interiorly focused autobiographical thinking* with I, me and mine as the primary focus. A healthy activity in this network may allow you to make a sense of the past, present and future. However, abnormal activity and connectivity in this network, particularly when the content is predominated by past losses or future uncertainties, correlates with negative mood and may be observed in several conditions including depression, anxiety, attention deficit, stress and autism. Early result suggests that excessive activity in the default network may even be associated with a predisposition to Alzheimer's dementia.

As a broad generalization, your attention at any moment is drawn by either the task positive network or the default network. **Optimal engagement of the task positive network and an ability to quiet the default network is the neuropsychological equivalent of complete and effortless focus with total immersion in the task at hand. This is a state of flow when you perceive minimal or no stress.**

If you are unable to appropriately quiet the default network, then you risk developing mind wandering and as a result, inattention to the present moment. In general, there are two situations when the default network is excessively engaged:

1) too many open files in your mind that you cannot close; or

2) not enough novelty in the world.

Think about when you are more likely to be lost in inwardly focused autobiographical thinking (also called the monkey brain). This will be more likely on days that are intense and challenging, particularly if the stressors cannot be easily resolved or are beyond control.

Mind wandering is also likely when your present moment does not offer much novelty. How exciting do you think is cooking mashed potatoes (for the thousandth time)?! Compare that to cooking some exotic tropical dish you have never made before for a special guest you adore. The latter would engage more of your mind and create more joy. Wouldn't it? It is when you are engaged in such novel activity that the default network becomes quieter.

Excess activity within the default network saps your energy and attention. Most of this time does not register in your awareness and is lost time generating what I like to call *"junk food of thoughts."* Part of training your mind and the brain is to learn how to (at least temporarily) close these extra open files. Further, this training also brings these ruminations in your awareness so they are shorter and less task impairing. In essence you reclaim a significant amount of lost time.

Studies show that we may be spending a third of our time every day stuck within the default mode. With disruptions in life, the time within the default mode further increases. This is lost time when you are mostly unaware of your presence. A significant part of this time can be reclaimed and experienced as enhanced present moment awareness.

With repeated experiences of stress, the lower limbic center and the default network become the predominant areas of activity in the brain. Thus stress becomes hardwired. The wonderful news is that these changes in the brain are reversible. Using a gift of nature to us, recognized recently by scientists as neuroplasticity, we can effect a change that hardwires us for resilience.

8. Stress (or resilience) hardwired

Over the last few decades scientists have carefully redefined the adaptability of the human brain. Unlike previous assumptions, our brain is remarkably plastic and in a constant state of change. This change is guided by how we use the brain—our perceptions and actions.

Stress hardwired

Consider a life that is governed by a constant feeling of imbalance between the demands and ability to meet those demands, lack of meaning, lack of control, and non-acceptance. Which parts of the brain do you think will be working over time in this state? The lower limbic center and the default network, isn't it?

Stress predisposes to excessive activity of the limbic center and the default network. Neurons within these parts of the brain proliferate, receive better blood supply and as a result, such a brain may lock one into unnecessary suffering. In such a state, the higher cortical center actually undergoes atrophy and becomes less efficient. Have you noticed a state of fog and sometimes memory impairment when you are stressed? Actually chronic excessive stress may even predispose a person to dementia. The wonderful news is that you have an option to reverse this process, by rightwiring your brain for resilience.

Resilience hardwired: the heartful brain

Just as stress can get hardwired in the brain over a period of time, you will be correct in surmising that resilience also can get hardwired. By cultivating more positive and rational thoughts, greater meaning, and better sense of control, higher cortical center strengthens, limbic center becomes quieter, the default network over activity subsides and the task positive network optimally engages. ***This process helps you develop a resilient heartful brain. Trained attention, forgiveness, acceptance, compassion, higher meaning, meditation and prayer all activate the higher cortical center of the brain.***

A heartful brain can be conceptualized as a resonating organ that has beautifully coordinated systems with optimal executive control of your attention and interpretations. The brain in this state has a fully engaged and empowered pre-frontal cortex and related areas and has a quiet limbic system that supports your well-being and happiness rather than intoxicating you with negative emotions.

A heartful brain has optimal balance between the right and left cerebral hemispheres and generates coordinated brain wave patterns. A heartful brain spends more time in task related activities rather than ruminating in the default network. The process of training and rightwiring your brain by awakening the higher cortical center, once initiated, perpetuates itself by a lovely feedback loop that operates in your brain. To put it simply: the trained mind activates the brain's higher cortical center and quiets the lower limbic center; activation of the higher cortical center in turn helps train your mind (Figure 8.1). By training attention and refining interpretations, you stop feeding energy to the limbic center. This quiets the limbic center and empowers the cortical center.

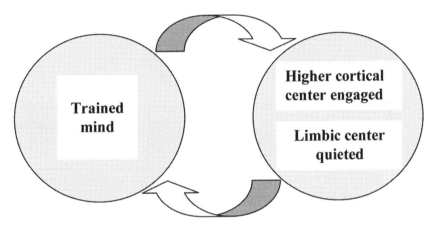

Figure 8.1 The feedback loop between training the mind and engagement of the higher cortical center and quieting of the lower limbic center

Your ability to deepen and prolong your attention and refine your interpretations provides the doorway to train your brain, engage your heart and transform your life. It is easy, doable, and worth the effort.

When your prejudices and egocentric preferences dominate your perception, they excessively engage and wrongly direct the content of interpretations. In this state, conscience-guided principles become subdued and the overload of negative interpretations keeps you surrounded by imperfections. You spend an inordinate amount of time in your mind away from the beautiful world.

At the level of the brain, the stress and attention deficit engendered in this process engages parts of the limbic system, particularly the amygdala, and suppresses the more evolved components, particularly the pre-frontal cortex. The innate systems and processes of your brain further increase your suffering, because once your limbic system gets fully engaged, it strengthens itself in a positive feedback loop. Almost every day I see people stuck in this state, sometimes for decades or even longer, because of this limitation in the functioning of our brains.

There is no doubt in my mind you have a way out.

The first step to come out of this process is to understand how it operates. Once you know its underpinnings, the knowledge will likely make you enthusiastic about learning ways to deeply and securely engage your attention in the world. You accomplish this by taking your attention out of your mind into the world and deepening and sustaining your attention by delaying judgment and finding novelty. This is how you invite joy within the mundane. You practiced this as a child, and as a result were able to live every day of your life to the fullest. ***You have to awaken that child within again if you wish to transform your life.***

Simultaneously with attention training, you refine your interpretations by bringing to them the attributes of gratitude, compassion, acceptance, forgiveness, and higher meaning and purpose to your life. Deeply nourishing relationships, meditation, and devotional prayer provide additional tools to refine your perceptions. You started developing these attributes, but the advancement may have stalled at some point, likely because of the vicissitudes of the modern world combined with the imperfections of the human mind and the brain. ***You have to discover and nurture that adult again.***

With these two steps, your engagement with life will be sound and secure. You will be unstuck from the limbic mode and excessive default network activity and will have engaged and empowered brain's higher center, the pre-frontal cortex and the task positive network.

Let us now turn to the first step in this program, attention training.

Section II: Attention Training

9. A unit of experience

Life can be described as a series of experiences. So analyzing a single unit of experience may be an optimal first step to develop insights into the workings of the mind. A unit of experience has three components: Attention; Interpretation; and Action (Figure 9.1)

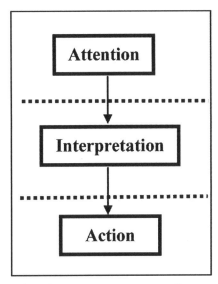

Figure 9.1 The three components of an experience

Attention is the first component. Attention opens the gateway that brings information into your mind. Once the sensory input is brought into your awareness, it is processed with the pre-stored information. This process leads to interpretations. Based on how you interpret the information, you decide on a particular course of action. Let us take the example of how you might look at a picture.

The image is first processed by the retina. From there through the optic nerve, the image reaches the brain (visual cortex). If you are distracted with your mind's eye looking elsewhere (preoccupied), you might not even register this image even though it is being projected on to the brain. To visualize this image, you have to purposefully pay attention to it, thereby engaging your mind (mind's eye) with the part of the brain where this image is registered. The sensory input brought in by attention is then integrated with the previously stored information, a meaning is assigned to it, and the whole process provides you an experience.

10. The mechanics of attention

Attention provides the entry point into your mind. If you do not pay adequate attention, then your conclusions are likely to be based on incomplete data and you are likely to misinterpret a lot of your sensory experience. Mechanistically, attention has three important aspects: direction, duration, and depth (3Ds)

1. Direction of attention: Attention could be directed toward the world or the mind. In general, untrained attention tends to be divided, with a proportion (usually a larger proportion) of attention directed toward the mind (Figure 10.1). For example, while driving to the office, part of your attention may be with the car and the road while the rest may be busy planning the day, or thinking about what happened yesterday or the day before. The tendency to be more in the mind is particularly exaggerated if you are burdened with several unresolved issues. These are the extra open files, lodged within the default network of the brain. **Many patients describe this to me as the feeling of a hamster running uncontrollably in their head.**

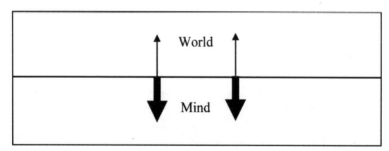

Figure 10.1 Untrained attention tends to be divided, with a higher proportion of the attention directed toward the mind

2. Duration and depth of attention: With respect to the duration and depth, attention is of two distinct types – *instinctive or purposeful. Instinctive attention* is our innate attention that often oscillates between attention deficit or hypervigilant focus. *Purposeful attention* is the trained attention that is focused, relaxed, altruistic, non-judgmental, in the present moment, sustained and purposeful. Majority of us use the innate instinctive attention for the larger proportion of the day (and life). This instinctive attention is guided by motivation. **Evolutionarily, this motivation is primarily provided by paying attention to threat or pleasure.** Paying attention to threat or pleasure has offered us survival advantage and is thus hardwired within us. Between threat and pleasure, it is the threat that captures greater part of our attention. This is true for infants as young as 7 months old.

3. The next question then is where can we find most of our threats and pleasures? In reality, the daily experiences within the world commonly miss on significant threat or extraordinary pleasure for most of us. Compared to a few thousand years ago, the cumulative threat coming from the world is much lower. Currently, our experiences on most days tend to be a repetition of previous days, most of our possessions and relationships remain similar and familiar from one day to the next. The world, thus, does not provide adequate anchor to keep our instinctive attention.

4. Our mind, however, is a store house of memories and experiences that need resolution. These are in the form of hurts and regrets (past), and desires and fears (future). These memories and experiences in the mind are augmented by our constant rumination about them. Rumination then leads to attempts to suppress the thoughts, the avoidant response. Attempts to suppress the thoughts, however, runs counter to its desired purpose. Thought suppression actually predisposes to even greater number of thoughts about the same event, just like the song that might play in your head some days. The more you try to suppress it, the stronger it gets. The whole process is fueled by your extraordinary ability to imagine. Everything that you imagine, your brain experiences as if it has already happened. Imagination is truly a double-edged sword. You use your power of imagination to think ahead, plan and create your beautiful world. However, if your imagination is focused on a negative event, you may experience several negative contingencies related to that event also. As Mark Twain cleverly said, *"I have been through some terrible things in my life, some of which actually happened."*

Thus memory of a hurt, combined with rumination about it, unsuccessful attempts toward thought suppression and your extraordinary ability to imagine generates attention-drawing sumps within the mind that I like to call "attention black holes" (ABHs) (Figure 10.2). Mind also carries pleasant memories and exciting anticipation of happy future events. Instinctively however, we are more drawn toward imperfections than positive events. For this reason and for the sake of simplicity, I will focus primarily on ABHs at this time.

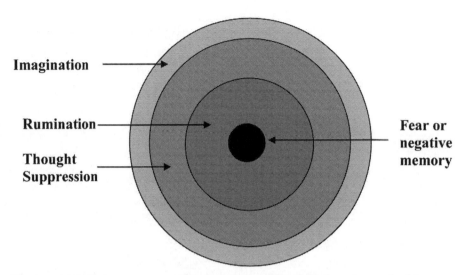

Figure 10.2 The anatomy of an attention black hole—kernel of fear or negative memory surrounded by layers of thoughts created by the mind, an avoidant response that in effect increases attention to the fear or negative memory and imagination.

5. Many of us might have multiple such attention black holes lodged within the mind (Figure 10.3). They are related to all the open files in our mind that we are not able to close. These draw our attention toward the imperfections of the past and the future within the mind, and away from the present moment of the world.

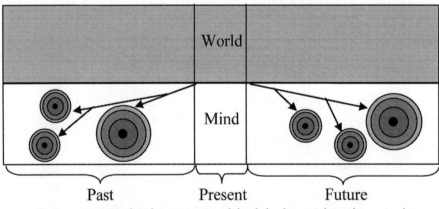

Figure 10.3 Multiple attention black holes within the mind

When several of these black holes impact our thinking, we are unable to quiet our mind easily—the hamster keeps racing uncontrollably. This exhausting process is the genesis of excessive amounts of stress.

With this state of the mind, the present moment often gets colored by these black holes. These black holes hijack our attention and thereby usurp a lot of energy, time and joy. They activate the default network and the lower limbic loop. The world may start seeming dull if you start living a larger proportion of your life in the mind in the company of these black holes. A constant company of hurts, regrets, desires, and fears increases the amount of stress, anxiety, and depression. This multiplies the time one may spend stuck within the survival mode, in the process activating stress responders in the body—with multiple adverse consequences.

So the schematic so far is:

- Our attention could be drawn toward world, mind, or both.
- Attention depends on motivation.
- Threats and pleasure serve as the primary motivators for our attention.
- World commonly misses on such tangible threats or pleasures (particularly extraordinary pleasures).
- Mind is a storehouse of attention-drawing memories and experiences.
- These are stored in the form of multiple attention black holes.
- Our attention is thus naturally and instinctively drawn toward these attention black holes that are within the mind.
- When in the mind, this attention gets stuck within the imperfections of the past and the future.
- We start living our life predominantly in the mind, often for no fault of ours.
- Constantly surrounded by hurts, regrets, desires, and fears, we may remain in a state of stress for longer than desirable.
- Over a period of time, the increased activity of the limbic loop and the default network hardwires us for an exaggerated stress response.

(Recognize that this process is ingrained within the systems of our brain and the mind. I am convinced that a large proportion of stress we experience on a daily basis is not a person's fault, but primarily originates in our untrained brain and mind's imperfections.)

6. Ideally one would want to have a mind completely free of any black holes. But that is unrealistic. An alternate and effective solution could be to train your attention so it is stronger and not easily pulled by the black holes. You can indeed train your attention just as you can train and strengthen a muscle in the body.

An important key question then is where do you think should the attention first be directed for this training?

Toward the world? ☐ /or
Toward the mind? ☐

Toward the world, isn't it?

Programs that train your attention by pushing you deeper into the mind may work for some of us, but are often inefficient and entail considerable time and effort. This is one of the reasons why meditation tends to be a difficult practice. *Going inward into the mind as a first step may be an appropriate approach if you live in a monastery, but does not work very well in the modern, fast-paced world.* I believe going deeper into the mind is an inefficient way to start training and stabilizing your attention and decrease stress. Unfortunately many current programs offer that as the primary approach, slowing down the progress. I believe in the present times, the more optimal approach is to train your attention so it does not fall an easy prey to the black holes. **In other words, train your attention to pull it out of the mind into the world.**

7. An essential step toward this solution is to impart to your attention three key characteristics:

> * Predominantly directed toward the world
> * Non-judgmental (or with delayed judgment)
> * Focused on novelty (I will elaborate the concept of novelty in Chapter 12)

Such a pattern of attention decreases stress and enhances the amount of joy, even within the mundane experiences. Hence, I like to call this pattern of attention, <u>Joyful Attention</u>.

Progressive cultivation of joyful attention draws your attention away from the mind and into the world. Once you stop feeding energy into the attention black holes, they gradually begin to dissolve. This dissolution and prevention from forming fresh attention black holes is accelerated by refining your interpretations.

At this point it will help to get a deeper understanding of how attention interacts with interpretations to create an experience. This understanding will help us develop a program of attention training.

11. Attention meets interpretation

As we saw above, attention ordinarily meets interpretation to create an experience. Let us work through an example.

Take a look at an ordinary pen. When you look at the pen your attention (x) (Figure 11.1) brings the sensory input into the brain to tell you that you are looking at a pen. At the same time your brain and mind have stored representation of how a pen should look like (y). These two impressions meet at a point giving you the experience; you figure out this is a pen.

Interpretation	(y)
	Attention (x)

Figure 11.1 Attention and Interpretation within the brain. Upward pointing slimmer arrow represents weak partially engaged attention; downward pointing thicker arrow represents dominating interpretation.

Once you figure out this is a pen, your attention no longer finds a reason to look at the pen any more. You move on to the next thing. This moving on is necessary and helpful and allows you to work with efficiency. However, there is one problem.

We tend to move on too fast and over deploy interpretations.

As we get older, we store countless rigid representations in our brain that provide a strong input wherein our attention is quickly disrupted by a strong interpretation. Once loaded with a sufficient number of these invariant representations, we stop paying attention to the world because we already "know" everything. Where is the need to look at the ordinary and the mundane? We still see the pen, but not this very pen. In this state, we might miss paying attention to many important and enjoyable aspects of our life, including even our loved ones. We forget that joy is in the details, the particulars, the specifics and not just in the biased generalizations.

Missing a "need" to pay attention to the world, we log off from the world. Our attention in this state is mostly directed toward the mind that is the storehouse of our attention black holes. The distribution of attention on a typical day in this state is shown below (Figure 11.2).

Mind   **World**
Figure 11.2 Distribution of attention on a typical day with the untrained mind

The figure below shows the nature of our attention in this state (Figure 11.3). Bulk of our attention is directed toward the mind, with a small proportion of attention toward the world. Such an attention predisposes to stress and anxiety.

Figure 11.3 Untrained attention is split between the world and the mind. In this state, bulk of the attention remains locked within the mind, switching from one thought to the next, decreasing your ability to pay attention to the world.

Once logged off from the world we have nowhere else to go but in our mind. In the mind, lurk attention black holes—we may, thus get lost within the imperfections of past and future. ***No matter how materially accomplished, I have seldom seen anyone sustain peace and happiness if they were predominantly living within their mind.***

A trained "purposeful attention" helps you pay greater attention to the world. This pulls your attention away from the mind and neurologically helps accomplish three objectives:

   * Engages and empowers your prefrontal cortex (PFC)
   * Helps you break the neural connections that constitute the attention black holes (Increased activity of the PFC (particularly the left PFC) correlates with happiness, well being, resilience, and extinction of negative memories)
   * Engage and strengthen the task positive network while quieting the default network

An important and pertinent question you might ask here is—we just said that the world does not have enough threat or pleasure to hold our attention? How can we then bring and engage our attention with the world? That is absolutely correct. Once we begin to take the world (including our loved ones) for granted, they do not easily hold our attention. With training, however, we cultivate a purposeful attention that no longer depends on threat or pleasure. This attention is now guided by the light of "novelty." We paid attention to this novelty as a child, but somehow the skill fades as we grow up. **Attention training entails waking up the child within you that can find novelty within the ordinary.** Let us look at few attention training exercises geared toward developing a trained attention by paying greater attention to novelty in our world and waking up the child within!

12. Attention training

Attention training entails cultivating a trained attention that has the following important characteristics:

- Predominantly directed toward the world
- Non-judgmental
- Seeks novelty

Cultivating purposeful attention will allow you to log back on to the world and savor it more fully. It isn't that you will not go into the mind at all. You still will. But you will go to a much lesser extent so your attention is fairly divided between the mind and the world (Figure 12.1).

Mind   **World**

Figure 12.1 Distribution of attention on a typical day in the attentive state
(compare with figure 11.2)

Another way of representing the same idea is in figure 12.2 below (compare with figure 11.3).

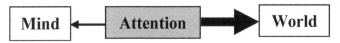

Figure 12.2 Trained purposeful attention is mostly with the world with little "attention dollars" invested in the mind

I will now present below two broad approaches to attention training that might help you take control of the direction, depth, and duration of the attention. ***The key component common to these skills is to find a way to synchronize your attention with your eyes and ears (and other senses) without developing a hypervigilant, anxious disposition.***

The two approaches are:
1. **Joyful Attention: Delay Judgment and Pay Attention to Novelty**
2. **Kind (saintly) Attention: Attend with Compassion, Acceptance, Love and Forgiveness**

12.1. JOYFUL ATTENTION:

DELAY JUDGMENT AND PAY ATTENTION TO NOVELTY

Remember the last time you saw a dance recital by a group of 3-year olds or basketball game of young boys. It is always a source of joy to watch the little ones perform.

Do you think their performances are polished and professional or pretty chaotic? Pretty chaotic, isn't it. Then why do we enjoy their performances so much? I think part of the reason is we do not judge them. We accept their performance for what it is. The very fact that they are on the stage is a reason for joy.

Now compare this experience with watching a professional football game. A very interesting study published in 2008 in the *New England Journal of Medicine* suggested that the day Germans were watching their own team playing in the 2006 world cup soccer, they experienced up to three times the risk of a serious acute cardiovascular event. Why should an entertaining activity mutate into a life threatening event? This to my mind is related to excessive judgments invested in each move of the game. Viewers often wish to control the flow and outcome of the game by watching the television screen and are frustrated at their inability to do so.

Both the experiences, watching little kids perform and play or watching a soccer match should ideally be a source of joy. But a lot depends on how you approach the event. If you relate with excessive judgment and bias, you could take the joy away and convert the experience into potentially a life-threatening event. When you delay judgment, you create an open receptacle to pay attention to novelty.

Before we start the attention training exercises, a word of caution: Please do not practice these exercises while driving, operating heavy machinery, or doing any other such activity that will be negatively affected by your attention being drawn away.

Let us begin the training by paying attending to a flower (Figure 12.3).

Figure 12.3 A flower

12.1.1 Seek Novelty:

Exercise #1. Take a quick superficial look at this flower and then read the text that follows.

All you might see is just another flower, nothing much special or exotic about it.

Now take another look. This time bring your full attention (and patience) in seeing this flower, as if you or your loved one painted it. Forget yourself for a moment and try to be fully immersed in the flower. Look at it with the intention of finding novelty in it.

Can you see that the petals are broadly arranged in two layers? See the separation between two adjacent petals starting at 12 o' clock position. Are they symmetrical or arranged a bit randomly? Look at each petal individually. Do you see that each petal has a unique shape and size? Do you see the lines on the surface of the petals that break them into three segments? Jagged edges? Is each jagged edge unique? Is the intensity of light reflected from the surface of the petals a bit unique for each of them? Do you realize that each petal might be an independent unit on its own?

Now look at the center of the flower. Do you see about a hundred stamens? How about the dark (beauty spot!) a little off center? I wish you were able to also feel this flower in your hand and experience its fragrance.

Clearly this flower is novel. There is no flower on planet earth exactly like this, there never was and never will be. This novelty however will only be perceptible if you purposefully make this flower the entirety of your world for a brief period of time.

One question I often ask learners is what is not happening when you are fully absorbed in the novelty of this flower? By attending to this flower at a deeper level, you have externally directed and stabilized your attention and are freed up from ruminations or worrying for a moment. You have given a pause to mind's propensity for constant thinking. You have engaged the task positive network and pulled yourself out of the default network. On numerous occasions I have noticed profound attention shifts among patients and learners while watching this flower (with resultant decrease in feelings of anxiety). With repeated such practice, your attention might come under your greater influence so you can deploy it to process what you choose rather than being driven by the whims of the mind.

Can you treat the world around you a bit like how you just treated this flower? Can you sprinkle such attention several times during the day? Can you bring this attention to your loved ones when you are with them? When you meet your loved ones at the beginning or end of the day, can you meet them as if you are meeting them after a long time? Each day, day after day.

We all crave for other's attention. By providing this attention to others, you can significantly enhance their (and your) quality of life. The exercise with the flower above introduces you to your attention so you can train it and then deploy this pattern of attention where it is most needed (with your loved ones, friends, colleagues, clients, patients etc.).

Your power of attention is a bit like your muscles—it can be made stronger by appropriate work out. At the level of the brain, this pattern of deeper attention automatically delays interpretations, enhances the intensity of your sensory input, and allows you to see the world in its full brightness. The process repeatedly deployed has one additional benefit: it helps you disengage from and ultimately disempowers attention black holes. Compare figure 12.4 below with figure 11.1 above.

Interpretation	(y)
	↑
	Attention (x)

Figure 12.4 Attention and Interpretation within the brain. Upward pointing, thicker arrow represents stronger engaged attention; downward pointing, thinner arrow represents trained interpretations.

Training attention takes a bit of effort, often a lot of effort. You also have to repeatedly remind yourself to sustain this pattern of attention. Unless you create a purposeful intention, attention black holes are likely to draw you within their folds. I will now present this core basic concept in different exercises to help you work toward strengthening your attention. Experience these exercises, identify the ones you find most appealing, and incorporate them in your daily schedule.

Exercise #2. Uniqueness within the ordinary

Pick four similar looking oranges (alternately apples, apricots, plums, potatoes, cucumber, or any other medium-sized vegetables or fruits will do). Look at these oranges as if you actually created them. Carefully study how the final product turned out. Look at their shape, size, color, fragrance, surface, weight, and all the undulations on their skin. Look at the uniqueness of the "Grand Canyons" (all the dimples) inscribed on each orange's surface.

Do you think despite their superficial similarity all the individual oranges are different, unique, and special in their own way? Do you think this is true for every fruit—every tree—every human—every life form? Are you missing something by failing to notice this novelty?

Ducks floating in the pond seem like a photocopy of each other. In a group, each penguin might also look identical to the others in shape, size, and color. Yet they are all individuals, have unique personalities, have their own families, a different voice, emotions, and responsibilities. So does an ant, a grasshopper, even a ladybug. If you were to adopt two ladybugs as pets, more than likely you will give them two different names! Next time you look at any of these cute creatures, try paying attention to their individuality. This is also true for every human being.

Every one of us is unique and novel in our own way. We have our own story. It is just a chance that some stories you know and others you don't. If you pay attention to novelty in an individual, without caging too much of that into good or bad, you might be fascinated by the variety and richness you learn. If you look for novelty, you will invariably find it. A search for novelty in the ordinary will increase your depth of attention and improve your observation.

Your ability to remain in the world depends on finding novelty within boring, extraordinary within ordinary. Novelty is not conditioned by duality. While generally appraised in a positive sense, novelty often is value neutral. I might find something novel yet not have an intention to acquire it. *Novelty is free of judgment or prejudice.* Novelty is pure appreciation of uniqueness. An item or an event does not have to serve the self for it to be novel. You often consider something novel if it is original, contrasting, unique, exclusive, and beyond usual expectation. Is it possible you are deluged with novelty all the time but are just failing to notice? My guess is that this is indeed the case. The world around us is suffused with novelty. As we grow older, we lose the ability to perceive it. With attention training, you wake up the child within you that can easily find and attend to the novelty within the ordinary.

An ability to find novelty independent of inherent value helps greatly with the depth of attention. To find novelty, you have to let go of mind's constant tendency to plan, problem solve, over categorize and ruminate. **When I find my mind ruminating, I often tell myself, "For the next 10 minutes I have nowhere to go, nothing to accomplish, nothing to plan, no problem to solve. I just have to be. The immediate world connected to my senses is my entire universe, no more no less."** It is very relaxing and nourishing to be in this state, both for myself and for others who I am with.

Let us do three additional exercises with novelty.

Exercise 3. Unique clothes

Pick your child's (or grandchild's or someone else's) dress. Look for novelty in this dress— see the cute buttons, the color patterns, appreciate the softness of the cloth, the baby fragrance, and all else your senses allow you to perceive. Look at this dress as if you are an expert at designing clothes.

Exercise 4. Sea of novelty

Look around the house. Find novelty in your toothbrush; see the uniqueness in the apple you eat; find what is special about a flower, even a weed. Look with a fresh, open, and learning attitude at ordinary items in your home such as the door, windows, micro-wave, dishwasher, oven, furniture, bed, toothpaste, soap, and television. Each of these items has an element of uniqueness and novelty to it. Most of the things in your car, on the road, at work, or in restaurants are novel.

Would you agree that you are swimming in a sea of novelty? To appreciate this novelty you will have to delay value-based categorizations. Everything is as it is—magical, unique, and precious. Even the most mundane object is a product of fourteen billion years of work of the universe and is thus novel. Finding novelty helps you respect and adore the object of your attention. Just like the objects around you, and even more so, every individual you meet has a part of him or her that is unique and thus novel that you can notice, admire, and learn from.

Exercise 5. Novelty in individuals

Next time you meet someone at home or work, pay extra attention to their words. Attend to their novelty. Ponder on the amazing journey they may have travelled to present themselves in your life.

Once you are able to find novelty within the ordinary, you will be able to delete the word "boring" from your dictionary. Your propensity to pay attention to the contents of the mind will also decrease.

An important reminder here—by choosing to start the program of training attention, you are delving into a life-long learning program. On the surface, this seems like a simple straightforward skill. But in reality, it is the most engaging (and rewarding) challenge you may have ever taken.

Several additional approaches might help your ability to find novelty. Below I present four additional ideas to help your efforts toward training attention and discovering novelty that might otherwise elude the untrained eye.

12.1.2 Use one sensory system at a time:

A useful way of deepening attention is to attend to the object using a two-step process. In this approach, you first appreciate the object with all the senses working together. As a second step, you pay attention using one part of the sensory system at a time.

Exercise 6. Use one sensory system at a time

Pick an apple. Examine it as a two-step process;

Step 1 – Hold the apple in your hands and appreciate it as a whole.
Step 2 – Now appreciate the apple using your senses, one at a time.
1. *First "look" at the apple. Attend to its shape, color, its stem, and all the marks on it. Maybe there is a sticker describing where it was produced or packaged. Appreciate the uniqueness of this apple. There is probably no other apple in the world that is identical to this one in all its attributes.*
2. *Now engage your sense of touch and feel the apple. Feel its smoothness as well as all the corrugations and marks on its surface.*
3. *At this point bring this apple closer to your nose and take a deep breath of its fragrance. Savor this breath for a moment.*
4. *Keeping the awareness of the apple in your mind, close your eyes and imagine the apple is filled with empty space. Imagine this entire space. Imagine the space gradually filling with white soothing light.*
5. *Open your eyes, take the first bite of the apple, and close your eyes again. Feel the taste of the apple in your mouth and try to gently suck any juice that comes out of it. Once the juice stops flowing chew once and again enjoy the taste and suck the juice that gets released. Repeat this for a total of five chews. You can finish off the last pieces of this bite and then take the second bite of the fruit, repeating the exercise until the apple is all gone.*

Note two specific observations with this exercise:

1. The exercise may have introduced you to the uniqueness of the apple. You may realize that each apple has attributes of its own that are unique and precious.
2. The uniqueness can be more effectively ascertained if you use one sensory system at a time.

You can do this exercise with any other fruit or vegetable you like. Can you appreciate other aspects of your environment using one sensory system at a time? This is an excellent approach to train your attention and bring it back to the world.

12.1.3 Find one new detail (FOND):

The above two exercises (paying attention to novelty and using one sensory system at a time) are excellent to practice in the quiet of a room when you are by yourself. They will also help immediately bring your focus into the present and in the world anytime you find yourself mindless. A pragmatic version of these exercises, particularly in a familiar environment, is the FOND exercise. In this approach you attend to an object until the point that you are able to discern at least one new detail that you did not know previously.

Exercise 7. Find one new detail – The FOND exercise

Find four small objects that are familiar to you. If you cannot easily find four objects, use the four fingers of your right hand. Straighten these fingers and first study them as a whole and individually. Now try to discern the following four new details about your fingers you may not have paid attention to previously:

- *Compare the length of the index and ring fingers, which one is longer? (Hint – it varies between individuals)*
- *Does the tip of the little finger cross the second joint line of the ring finger or not quite so? (Hint – it varies between individuals)*
- *Can you individually fold any of the fingers and touch the surface of the hand, while keeping the other three fingers straight? (it may not be possible to do so— the fingers are connected to each other and do not like to move alone)*
- *Now turn your hand and look at the root of the nails. Which of the nails have a semi-lunar white area at the base?*

Did you learn a few new details about your fingers with this exercise?

If you picked four familiar objects such as a cell phone, pager, pen, and button on the shirt, find one detail that you did not know before about each object. For example:

- *What specific words are displayed when you turn on your cell phone?*
- *Do you have seconds displayed with the time in your pager?*
- *Is the make of the pen written in italicized or normal font?*
- *What is the color of the buttons on your shirt?*

The FOND exercise will not only make you more aware of your world, with familiarity, you are also likely to become fonder of things around you. As a result you will learn more, find it easier to remain out of the mind, and potentially have lower stress. FOND exercise is particularly helpful when you are in a familiar environment and is another way to make the world around you a bit more interesting. While the exercise is designed for just one new detail, you can attempt to find any number of details you consider appropriate.

Before we go to the next exercise, think about when during the day can you seek novelty, use one sensory system at a time, or find one new detail. Can you practice one of these approaches while getting ready in the washroom, loading the dishwasher, doing laundry, arranging clothes, eating, while watching TV, or talking to your friends or your loved ones? It will help to purposefully practice these exercises several (four to eight) times during the day to train your attention. Consider attention training along the same lines as you would consider physical workout. In Chapter 14, we will formulate these practices into a structured program that you can incorporate in daily life in such a way that the exercises end up saving time rather than costing any additional time.

12.1.4 Contemplate on the Story

So far, each exercise and concept has been directed to bring your attention to the outside world. The exercise discussed next is an exception that is a mix of remaining with the world, yet gingerly entering the mind.

Exercise 8. An apple's journey

Hold an apple in your hand. Give it a name, say "Applina." Become mindful of Applina by attending to her with all your senses individually. Now look at Applina and allow yourself to imagine her story. Right from a little insecure blossom on a tree in an orchard, Applina has had a successful career. Take your imagination to the orchard—to the tree, the branch, and the blossom from which Applina started. Imagine the span of time that has elapsed between that time and now. Imagine the space that separates you from that orchard.

The blossom was able to avoid the vagaries of the wind and the rain. It also survived the onslaught of insects and any number of other threats that could have destroyed it. Slowly the fruit evolved, from a small rancid baby apple to now a fully grown apple of this size. When ripe, Applina was picked by a person, labeled, stored, waxed, and then transported—probably thousands of miles away. In her journey with her friends, she was sometimes buried and uncomfortable, and at others on the surface and breathing fresh air. Imagine traveling with Applina in her journey. The journey across the country may have given Applina a few marks on her surface.

Finally having arrived at a grocery store, she was evaluated and placed for purchase. Applina wished to be bought before she became old and perished. Fortunately you found value in her and purchased her for the advertised price. She is now ready to fulfill her promise, willing to sacrifice herself for your nourishment.

Being eaten completes Applina's journey. This is exactly what she wants, but with one caveat—to be eaten mindfully. She has worked extremely hard all this while with one focus—to bring you nourishment. All she wants in return is that you enjoy each bite of her. This is how you pay respect to her—to each apple you eat—in fact, to everything you eat. This is the basic precept of mindful eating.

Every single item around you has such an amazing story that converges to one person—you. Bring your attention to all that surrounds you, take a pause, and contemplate on how each of the things have manifested in your life. Things like adhesive tape, pencil, pen, paper, pager, cell phone, toys, clothes, car, and many more. Hundreds of thousands of people may have worked together to bring you simple every day items. If you cultivate an ability to contemplate on the story, you may develop a skill to learn a deeper reality and pay greater attention because of a newfound respect for everything. The skill will also help you avoid rushing to judgments and refine your ability to try and understand others. Such attention makes everything seem special and flowers the kindness that is an inherent part of you. This is a particularly important attribute to carry for your loved ones and friends.

The fact that a particular group of friends and loved ones have presented themselves in your life is a miracle. If the life of the universe was one year, then humans arrived on December 31 at 11:59 P.M. and almost at the last second. With the universe so big and so old, and six and a half billion of us on planet earth, the probability that a particular group of individuals are present in your life is unimaginably small—certainly lower than winning a big lottery. Every human being connected with you represents a true miracle. Consider every relationship, at home or at work, a true blessing, a gift that you might treasure.

With your ability to contemplate on others' journey, you might realize that most people and things you encounter, you do somewhere in the middle of their journey. You meet your parents, your spouse, and your friends in the middle of their lives—you do not know their beginning and may not know their end. Most items in your home you know in the middle—not the beginning and probably also not the end. It is only when you pay attention to them and contemplate their story as they tell it that you can understand their unique preciousness and complete story. Most of what you own today was previously someone else's and will belong to another person after you pass it on. The purpose of knowing this is to realize the reality of impermanence of most things in your life. This realization will likely allow you to appreciate everything around you even more. It will help you develop altruism and its practical application—daily kindness. One way to radiate this kindness is by developing a kind attention.

2. KIND (SAINTLY) ATTENTION:

Attend with Compassion, Acceptance, Love and Forgiveness (CALF)

How do you think a self-actualized person interacts with the world? I think they forever are sending compassion, acceptance and love to every life form. Can you cultivate such an attention? The answer is yes and is the natural next step—to cultivate saintly attention that is effortlessly sending out compassion, acceptance, love and (where needed) forgiveness. To develop this attention, you have to train your eyes as organs that receive energy and also one that send out energy. Here is how to do it.

Generally when we see someone, we pay attention to their physical characteristics, exclude threat, focus on how attractive they are etc. Sometimes this attention pattern has a judgmental element to it. I believe we lose precious opportunity with this attention style. **To cultivate a kind attention, spend the first few moments of looking at someone as a precious time of sending compassion, acceptance, love and (where needed) forgiveness.** Your attention flows as a two-way process—when you see someone, as you imbibe their information, you send them a silent message of CALF. This is depicted in the figure below (Figure 12.5).

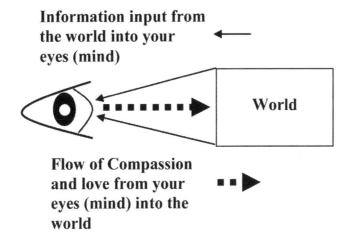

Information input from the world into your eyes (mind)

World

Flow of Compassion and love from your eyes (mind) into the world

Figure 12.5 Bidirectional attention: Send positive energy of Compassion, Acceptance, Love, and Forgiveness (CALF) as you pay attention to the world

A simple way to practice this exercise is to align your heart and eyes when you first see someone and send them a silent *"I wish you well"* or *"Bless you."*

Exercise 9. Silent "I wish you well"

To the first twenty people you see/meet today, send a silent "I wish you well" or "Bless you." See how you feel at the end of this practice. Try to repeat it tomorrow, the day after, and the following days.

Sending silent blessings to the world might benefit you in many ways:

1. You generally cannot give something you do not have. So in an effort toward sending the blessings, you will generate them within your being;

2. When you are generating blessings within yourself, it is very difficult (almost impossible) to have negative emotions at the same time;

3. You will likely keep part of the positive energy you generate;

4. Over a period of time, people receiving your silent blessings begin to recognize them; a process that might have remarkably positive effect on your relationships; and

5. The positive presence and blessings you share eventually reflect back to you.

13. Benefits of attention training

Your ability to sustain a deep attention in the world might have the following beneficial effects:

1) By learning to purposefully attend, you develop skills to choose attention at will;
2) Your ability to access and train different depths of attention helps you develop attention flexibility;
3) Since paying attention is a function of the pre-frontal cortex, you train your higher cortical center of the brain;
4) By anchoring attention in the world, your attention is not drawn toward the contents of your mind;
5) By anchoring attention in the world, you stop feeding energy to your attention black holes, thereby gradually disempowering them;
6) By deepening attention you delay interpretations, thus increasing the purity of sensory experience;
7) You learn more about the world by paying attention; and
8) When you learn to pay attention with the exercises presented, the skills you learn translate into other aspects of your life including improved ability to pay attention to your work, loved ones, and other aspects of daily living.

The fast-paced world today, overwhelming number of choices, and excessive exposure to the internet is making our attention weak and superficial. Internet works as a repository of rich information that is available to us at our fingertips. This decreases our need to remember. Further we have developed a habit of scanning for the most salient information from each webpage rather than reading the full text. Studies suggest most users spend only 15-20 seconds with each web page. With so many of us spending eight or more hours every day in front of the computer, our brain is likely deeply impacted by this experience, weakening our attention. In some ways, we now forage for information as hunter gatherers used to forage for food.

Weak and superficial attention cannot support a fulfilling life replete with joy and higher values. Exercise of compassion, acceptance, forgiveness and gratitude needs deeper attention. Attention training to my mind thus is an extraordinarily important skill to negate the effects of the fast-paced world on our brains.

Joy in an experience is associated with engagement of the task-positive network. If you enjoy fly fishing, golf or even bungee jumping, it is because each of these experiences engages a deeper attention and brings you into the present moment.

You cannot spend most of your life practicing these sports. You can, however, bring the same attention pattern to ordinary activities of the day. Very likely such attention will enhance your joy.

Training attention is about training an essential skill to be able to find joy within the ordinary. It is really treating your own being with compassion, acceptance, love and kindness.

14. Integrating attention skills

Let us integrate the skills we have discussed so far to create a practical and time-efficient program that you can embody each day. I am respectful and aware of how busy you are. Hence this program does not ask of you to take extra time away from work or play. Instead these exercises are integrated within your daily routine.

Central to the training is your intention to enhance the strength and quality of signal you receive from the world so you can engage with it at a deeper level. You are intending to cultivate an attention that is focused, relaxed, altruistic, non-judgmental, in the present moment, purposeful and sustained. This training generally progresses in two phases: **Train it and Sustain it.**

* Phase 1: Train it – this phase may last anywhere from 4-weeks to 24-weeks depending on your innate attention strength and how much effort you put in the training. A few specific skills that might help (and are described above) are:

     1.1 Seek novelty
     1.2 Use one sensory system at a time
     1.3 Find one new detail (FOND)
     1.4 Contemplate on the story
     1.5 Attend with CALF

I realize that in your busy life it may be challenging to sustain this pattern of attention all through the day. So here is your attention prescription.

Attention Prescription:

Find four (to eight) times during the day wherein you can safely and effectively practice an attention that is focused, relaxed, altruistic, non-judgmental, in the present moment, sustained and purposeful. Each of these practice times could be 15-20 minutes long. Optimal times for such practice include – waking up in the morning, breakfast, office meeting, presentation, lunch, arriving home from work, time with nature, dinner time, family time in the evening, prior to sleeping, in the church, and at a party. Add any other time that fits in well with your schedule. During these times remember to use both the attention skills – that of joyful attention and kind attention.

Let me share with you how I have worked toward training my attention and continually strive to do so.

The most vulnerable moment of my day is when I wake up in the morning. If I start my day with good control of attention, then I am more easily able to carry the momentum through the rest of the day. My morning attention exercise is primarily directed to delay the waking up of the hamster in my head. As soon as I wake up, it would love to get me busy in planning, problem solving, ruminating and worrying. I delay the process by giving my mind relaxing and nourishing alternatives.

As soon as I open my eyes in the morning, I start a simple exercise of prayerful gratitude by finding at least five things I could be grateful for this morning. My next focus is on five deep breaths, and then I bring attention to my body and feeling its stiffness give it a stretch. My dear hamster fights tooth and nail to draw me inside the mind (less so now than it used to before). But I gently tell it, not yet, since I have an appointment with myself in the early morning. As I step out of the bed, I try to feel the soft carpet beneath my feet. It is a comforting feeling. In the washroom when I turn the light on, I try to look at myself with kindness. While taking a shower, I do not allow my mind to travel to the breakfast table. Mind certainly gives it a try, but eventually gives up. I try to feel the water on my skin and pay attention to the rich fragrance of the soap and the shampoo. I feel connected to the river or creek from where this water may have come. As a result of this exercise, by the time I come out of the washroom, I feel more refreshed and energized than I used to. Using this simple routine has significantly enhanced the joy I perceive and the focus I am able to carry during the first half of the day. I think this is a great use of my time since in the past when I did not practice this exercise, I frequently experienced random chaotic ruminations (junk food of thoughts) resulting in stress and fatigue. You might ask, could I use this time for something more "productive?" May be or may be not. Personally I have never had profoundly enlightening realizations in the wash room! However, keeping my attention stabilized and centered has significantly enhanced my focus and joy during the first half of the day.

In the evening, as I pull my car into the garage, I try to forget that I am a professional. I am only a father, a husband, a friend or a son. I try to meet my loved ones as if I am meeting them after a long time. I try to relate to them with a genuine interest in knowing what has transpired in their lives since I last met them. I try to see the fresh novelty about them since I last saw them. I urge you to try this exercise for the next week and see if it impacts the quality of your evenings. An excellent approach might be to start looking at your loved ones with CALF when you start your evening.

Two additional specific times I suggest practicing this attention pattern during the day are with nature and during physical exercise. Physical exercise is a time for keeping the body active and mind relaxed. Try to be with the body and the environment while exercising and avoid too much planning or problem solving. I also suggest you spend at least 15 minutes every day with nature. Many of the man-made creations are emotionally dense. If you drive around downtown and see the displays on all the shops, they might create a little "want" in you. It is such unsatisfied wants that create unrest in the mind over a period of time. A tree however stands innocent, an emblem of calm, forever ready to give while asking nothing in return. Spend some time looking at the trees and the squirrels and birds finding a home on them. Research studies show that while we may spend a fair amount of time maintaining our yard, we seldom spend any time there. So if you have a yard in your home, you can practice such an attention while spending 15-20 minutes with nature.

Beyond the four to eight assigned times of practice, through the rest of the day, I try to maintain a purposeful presence in the world, particularly during the gaps that the day provides (such as standing in an elevator, in between seeing patients, etc.). Even during a conversation, I sometimes remind myself to bring a deeper attention toward the person I am talking to or send CALF their way.

When I feel a negative emotion related to some past or future contingency over which I have no control, I try to delay judgment and find a reason and meaning (both tangible and philosophical) behind it. I have noticed that during times of setbacks, negative ruminations can be significantly decreased by trying to send CALF or blessings to the world at that time and if possible, expanding the diameter of existence (in the larger context of the world, my personal problems are very small).

(Please note that I share my practice with utmost humility to provide you one approach that might help. In no way do I imply that I have developed an ideal attention pattern.)

Practicing this attention program will most likely not take any extra time from your schedule, particularly after the first few weeks of training. I like to look at it as adding sugar or chocolate powder to the milk. The volume remains about the same, yet the milk starts tasting a bit better (at least for some of us!). **Engaging with the world with a deeper attention might bring greater meaning and joy to your day while not burdening you with one more thing added to your to-do list.**

I have provided a daily journal in Appendix III that might help you follow a structured approach we use in our program. As you progress, you are ready to move to the sustain it phase.

* Phase II: Sustain it – After the initial training of 4 to 24 weeks, your active need for formal attention training using the skills discussed above might gradually decrease as you increasingly anchor into an attention pattern that is flexible, relaxed, altruistic, non-judgmental, in the present moment, purposeful and sustained. The need for formal practice time decreases because you are constantly in practice all through the day. The rate of progress is very individual. **Your goal is to advance from a transient state of calm and joy to a transformed stage wherein your innate trait sustains calm and joy most of the day.**

As you progress and achieve a more stable attention, I would still encourage you to keep yourself self-regulated with a basic daily practice. By this time, you will be much better attuned with your particular needs and will be able to carve out a program that best fits with your life.

Generally, around this time, I encourage learners to introduce 15-30 minutes of daily deep breathing program or an approach to incorporate progressive muscular relaxation or guided imagery. I have provided one suggested approach for this program in Appendix IV.

15. Summary

As this point in order to consolidate our understanding, I will summarize the entire theme in the next few pages. Please pause and reflect on each fact prior to proceeding to the next one. Start with the first and most important self affirmation:
I will not postpone joy.

15.1. Brain, its two centers and two networks

Your brain has two groups of centers that are directly related to stress and resilience:

* The higher cortical center – When optimally activated, decreases stress and helps you be calm, happy, joyous, and resilient
* The lower limbic center – When activated, increases stress and makes you anxious, unhappy, depressed, and stressed

Your brain has two networks of operation:

* The task-positive network – This is engaged in externally focused activities. Its optimal engagement generally is associated with the feeling of "flow" and a state of joy.
* The default network – This is engaged in internally-focused thinking. Its excessive engagement generally is associated with negative ruminations and worrying and predisposes to stress, anxiety, depression and mind wandering with resulting attention deficit.

The simple rule of the brain is: If you engage a part of the brain, you empower it for the future. The brain, thus can change in response to experience, a phenomenon popularly called neuroplasticity.

* Greater use of the cortical center makes the cortical center stronger
* Greater use of the limbic center makes the limbic center stronger
* Greater engagement of the task-positive network makes the task-positive network stronger
* Greater engagement of the default network makes the default network stronger

You have a choice to engage and empower one or the other brain center and networks.

Compassion, acceptance, forgiveness, higher meaning and purpose, having a closely knit tribe, meditation, prayer, and healthy lifestyle activate the cortical center.

15.2. The Mind

The mind is the sum total of the processes that lead to perceptions and actions

Your mind influences all aspects of your perceptions

Perceptions have two components: Attention and Interpretation

15.3. Attention

Attention allows you to register, imbibe and transmit the information for processing

Research shows that human attention latches on to threat, pleasure, or novelty (TPN)

World offers some TPN, but often not enough to engage our attention. Our daily experiences are often repetitive (even boring); as a result we may fall into inattention with respect to the world.

Inattention to the world pushes us into the mind

Mind harbors attention black holes that strongly draw your attention

These black holes form as a result of previous or anticipated negative experiences potentiated by rumination, imagination, and an avoidance response. Our primary tendency to focus on the negative (negativity bias) strengthens these black holes.

Attention buried in the black holes saps your time, energy and joy

Time spent within the mind may entangle you into an exhaustive journey into the past and future in a mindless state of excessive and negative thinking

While you are within the mind, the world keeps progressing at sixty seconds / minute. You might thus be disengaged from the present moment. Days may become dull and drab, and full of stress.

15.4. Interpretations

Information collected by the process of attention is mixed with the principles and prejudices to generate interpretations

"Untrained" interpretations tend to be guided by prejudices

Excessive and prejudiced interpretations make our thinking pattern excessively self-seeking

Such interpretations cut short attention. Attention is also negatively affected by the fast-paced world, availability of multiple choices, and excessive exposure to the internet. The cumulative effect is that attention becomes superficial and fleeting.

Superficial weak attention and prejudiced interpretations engineer a stressful self-focused life.

15.5. The Two Steps
Training Attention and Refining Interpretations constitute the two key steps.

Step one: Train your attention

* Deepen your attention by training the direction, duration, and depth of your attention as discussed above
* This takes away the attention deficit and helps you attain attention balance
* It pulls you out of the mind into the world
* Trained attention makes it easier for you to engage with the present moment
* Training attention trains and strengthens the innate attention capacity of your brain
* Trained attention gives you the ability to think deeply and better handle complexity

Step two: Refine your interpretations

* Delay your interpretations (judgment)
* Wisely choose between the principles and prejudices to interpret
* Whenever possible, base your interpretations on principles-based values rather than prejudices
* The five core values are gratitude, compassion, acceptance, forgiveness, and meaning and purpose

Trained attention and interpretations help you attain a state of *heartfulness*. Heartfulness is defined as, *"Enhancing present moment awareness and experiencing it with greater gratitude, compassion, acceptance, forgiveness, and higher meaning and purpose."*

15.6. The trained brain and engaged heart
Trained attention and refined interpretations awaken the brain's higher cortical center and may engage the task positive network and quieten the default network. This makes the brain more heartful.

An engaged and empowered higher cortical center and task-positive network, and quieter default network may make it incrementally easier to deepen attention and refine interpretations

Inviting a tribe around you, meditation, prayer and healthy life style also engage the higher cortical center

The trained brain, trained attention, and refined interpretations support the inner core of peace, joy, and resilience

The process leads to transformation, an advanced stage wherein you may experience sustained peace and joy and progress toward self actualization

Thank you for paying attention to your attention!

The next step…

The information imbibed by your mind is integrated in the brain with your innate preferences, principles and sometimes prejudices to create your interpretations. Attention and interpretations work together to generate your perceptions and experiences. The next section will cover the second aspect of the AIT and SMART program, training interpretations. In brief you will learn to decrease instinctive, prejudice-based, excessive interpretations and instead offer yourself higher principles-based values of gratitude, compassion, acceptance, forgiveness, and meaning and purpose.

See you there!

Section III:
Interpretations Training

Information collected by the process of attention is admixed with our principles and prejudices to generate interpretations. "Untrained" interpretations tend to be guided by prejudices. Excessive and prejudiced interpretations make our thinking pattern excessively self-seeking. Such interpretations cut short attention. Attention thus becomes superficial and fleeting. Prejudiced interpretations predispose to a stressful self-focused life.

In our efforts toward training interpretations, you will learn to wisely choose between the principles and prejudices to interpret. You will learn that to the extent possible you should base your interpretations on principles-based values rather than prejudices. **The five core values are gratitude, compassion, acceptance, forgiveness, and meaning and purpose.**

16. Integrating interpretation skills

I am certain you all have a basic familiarity with the core values of gratitude, compassion, acceptance, forgiveness, and meaning & purpose. So as a first step, let us try to integrate the interpretation skills into a daily program. We will then discuss each of these values as the next step.

A very effective approach I have found is to keep a daily theme with the following suggested sequence:

Monday's theme:	**Gratitude**
Tuesday's theme:	**Compassion**
Wednesday's theme:	**Acceptance**
Thursday's theme:	**Meaning and Purpose**
Friday's theme:	**Forgiveness**
Saturday's theme:	**Celebration**
Sunday's theme:	**Reflection / Prayer**

Let me share with you how I try to apply these themes to my life.

On Mondays, I focus on gratitude. I start my day with five thoughts of gratitude and throughout the day, particularly when my attention is pulled by the default network of my brain particularly with a negative focus, I try to actively practice gratitude. Walking among patients through the hallways on a Monday, my first thought is gratitude—for their trust and the respect they accord to our profession. Toward colleagues and fellow care providers, I focus on gratitude for their kindness. I feel gratitude toward my wife for being such a good anchor for our family. I try to change my inner and outer dialog using gratitude as the central theme.

On Tuesdays, the day of compassion, first thing in the morning after five thoughts of gratitude, I focus on three thoughts of compassion—for someone I love, for someone I barely know and for someone I find difficult to love. I focus on the reality that all of us experience suffering of one form or the other, are fighting a little or a large battle in our life and thus deserve causeless compassion from each other. This is particularly so for patients who might feel vulnerable and often have a sense of lack of control, uncertainty, or the realization of finiteness. It is, thus appropriate to harbor instinctive natural compassion for everyone. A simple way I practice compassion through the day is by sending a silent "bless you" to people I happen to meet. Compassion allows kindness to flow more easily and fully.

On Wednesdays, I focus on acceptance, primarily living the day accepting myself as I am and accepting others as they are. At its core, acceptance helps me delay judgment and allows time for the higher centers of the brain to engage which is particularly helpful when I process an unpleasant event. Acceptance allows me to be kind, fair and rational even in the middle of a day that may have invited chaos. Acceptance fosters inner equanimity which stops me from fighting myself and saves considerable energy to respond to the external challenge.

Thursday is the day of meaning and purpose. On this day, I focus on the primary long-term meaning and purpose of my life, which is to be an agent of service and love. On Thursdays, I focus more on the energy that I should send to others rather than on the energy that might or might not be coming my way. Something akin to what John F. Kennedy said, *"Ask not what your country can do for you; ask what you can do for your country."* So Thursday is the low expectation day, a day of humility. It is the day to be pleasantly surprised and excited about each packet of energy coming your way. Pleasure is easier to find if you can decrease the threshold of what will make you happy.

Friday is the day of forgiveness. I start this day forgiving anyone who might hurt my feelings today. I also forgive myself for my past mistakes, known and unknown. By starting the day with the commitment of forgiveness for self and others, I am less self conscious and more accepting of any critique (with related opportunity for growth) that comes my way. If a learner has a significant hurt related to a previous transgression, I suggest they be slow and deliberate in their progress in forgiveness and focus on living just one day a week (i.e. Friday) in forgiveness.

Saturday is the day of celebration and Sunday of reflection and prayer. Celebration and prayer are related to your individual lifestyle and beliefs so I will not go into greater specifics regarding the same. Suffice it to say that keeping a general flavor of altruism is likely to enhance peace, joy and resilience, through work as well as play.

Am I able to perfectly practice what I just described above? Certainly not. But do I think I am much better than I was may be a decade ago? Absolutely. The progress is often slower than desirable, but progress it is nonetheless. And with this progress comes the gifts of freedom (from the mind), greater joy and better self-control.

If you keep these themes with you through the day as suggested, you will start doing ordinary things extraordinarily. **Character is more determined by how you relate with the common and mundane and not particularly when the spotlight is on you.**

A few self affirmations I find useful to remember particularly in the morning are summarized below:

- Gratitude: I am grateful for all that this day will bring
- Compassion: I will be compassionate toward everyone I meet today; I will treat myself with kindness today
- Acceptance: Everyone I meet today I will try to accept them just as they are; I will live the day today accepting myself just as I am
- Higher Meaning: I will live the day today by the higher meaning in my life
- Forgiveness: I will try to forgive anyone who might hurt my feelings today; I forgive myself today for my past mistakes

You might ask, why not practice gratitude on Tuesday also. The purpose of providing a structured approach is to have a particular focus for each day and is not directed to exclude other values. **In fact with practice, you will realize that each of these values converge toward the same point. They are different flavors of one core value—that of love.**

Further, the suggested practice is not intended to be nerdy or make you rigid. If you find a particular skill difficult to practice, you can substitute it for another that is easier to embody. Some learners have shared with me that they primarily practice gratitude the entire week. That is just fine. What we have here is a roadmap. You can carve out your journey the way you like. But if you have no particular reason to choose otherwise, I would suggest you to at least start with this sequence.

At an early stage in practice, you might use these values as a way to reinterpret your negative experiences and thereby decrease negative ruminations and emotions. They are your quarterbacks. As you advance, they may become the defining aspect of your day. The whole day may become one constant stream of gratitude, compassion, acceptance, higher meaning or forgiveness. How can suffering find a home in such a being?

In the rest of this section we will look at each of these values in greater depth.

17. Gratitude (Grateful Mondays)

Gratitude represents acknowledging the blessings you have received or might receive and feeling/showing appreciation for the same. Gratitude is your moral memory and is a combination of humility, grace, love, and acceptance.

It is useful to draw a distinction between gratitude and indebtedness. Indebtedness is an expectation created because of the benefits you may have received so you could reciprocate back in kind. Indebtedness may make you feel heavy; you may feel weighed down by the help you have received. Gratitude is a much purer feeling. Gratitude is not outcome dependent and originates primarily in the intention. It is not a result of benefit, it is a positive attitude. Gratitude creates no expectations and has no fear, hierarchy or desire. Gratitude is not expressed to receive more. Gratitude is a pure state of being, an expression of love for being treated with grace and compassion. You have gratitude not only for what people do, but simply for who they are. Gratitude helps you be thankful for every experience life brings to you, good or bad, realizing that every experience provides you an opportunity to learn and grow.

Gratitude fosters humility and helps you decrease your ego. Gratitude helps you find miraculous within the ordinary. Deep honest gratitude is a wonderful prayer. Gratitude takes you toward freedom, from both cravings and aversions. This is true wisdom.

Exercise 1. Say "thank you" in the morning

When you wake up each morning, even before you open your eyes, think of five things you could be grateful for and spend the first thirty seconds silently expressing gratitude. These could be such simple things as a soft carpet, a warm room, a good night's sleep, toothpaste, electricity in your home; or might include people around you such as your spouse, children, friends, or siblings; or even gifts of touch, vision, faith, or anything else that might come to your mind. All these are true blessings that we tend to take for granted.

Exercise 2. Say "thank you" during the day

At least once every day find a reason to express appreciation to someone. You could do this by sending a card, a gift, a favorable e-mail, or just plain heartfelt words of "thank you." If none of these are feasible on a given day, you could send a silent thank you message to them.

Exercise 3. Say "thank you" at night

As you close your day prior to your sleep, find at least one thing you could be thankful for that day.

Exercise 4. Gratitude exercise with children

Try this exercise with your children, grandchildren or friend's children for practicing gratitude as well as exercising their brain. Ask them to note three things they are thankful for starting with a letter of each alphabet (A to Z). For each thing or person, ask them why the particular thing or person is important to them.

Kindly remember: Gratitude with an attitude is not gratitude; what you need is an attitude of gratitude!

18. Compassion (Compassionate Tuesdays)

Compassion (co = together; passion = strong feeling; to suffer with) is your ability to feel the suffering of others—often with a desire to help. Empathy, a closely related term is your capacity to understand another person's experience from within their perspective. Compassion finds its origin in the golden rule, *"Do unto others as you would have them do unto you."*

Your ability to find a common ground with the other person helps with your compassion. Often even a similarity in experience and being able to identify with what the other is going through can help with compassion.

In truth all of us are fighting a little (or larger) battle in our lives. A vast majority of us experience negative emotions each day. We often cannot see others' suffering because while we can feel our inside, we can only perceive others' outside. Just as life is simpler if you always speak the truth, I think life is simpler if your innate state is to harbor compassion for everyone. This is particularly true when you find your loved ones, friends or colleagues frustrated or upset. One belief that has transformed my relationships can be expressed as, ***"An expression other than love is often a call for help."***

In fact I believe that an expression of anger or frustration almost always is a call for help. Anger, hatred, jealousy all represent an inner void not accepted. With such a void and in ignorance, we mistakenly may attempt to fill our own inner emptiness by creating emptiness in someone else. Understanding this truth will provide you numerous benefits.

You will feel so much better about yourself when your first reaction to someone who seems upset is that they are hurting in some way. Their frustration is not about you or them, it is some true genuine inner conflict they are not able to resolve. This belief will lead to a search for the reason they are hurting. More often than not, you will be able to find a rational explanation for the same. The result—lesser reactive frustration on your part and as a result more mature response; better ability to solve the primary issue at hand; more meaningful relationships; better self esteem for them and you; and in the long-term, lower likelihood of their being upset again. The first step in this process is to truly believe that *an expression other than love is indeed a call for help*.

Let us do a few compassion exercises:

Exercise 1. Compassion for someone you love

Sit in a safe place with your eyes closed. Draw an imaginary circle. Place yourself in that circle. Within that circle also include someone you dearly love. Create positive warm feelings for that person.

Now focus on how the two of you are similar. At its most basic level you are both humans. You have similar biologic needs (food, breath, healthy body). You both need love, care, and security. Next find other areas of similarities. Do you have similar preferences for food? Do you both like to travel? Do you both have unique idiosyncrasies? Do you like similar clothes? Are your movie choices similar? Try to find similarities even in differences. Are you both similar in having unique preferences?

Now with each in breath imagine that you are sharing their pain and suffering. With each out breath imagine sending them healing energy and love.

The more similarities you seek and are able to find, the closer you will come to others, including your loved ones. You are then more likely to accept their uniqueness, even those aspects that so far may have seemed annoying.

Exercise 2. Compassion for someone you barely know

Sit in a safe place with your eyes closed. Draw an imaginary circle. Place yourself in that circle. Within that circle, allow yourself to include someone you barely know. Create positive, warm feelings for that person.

Now focus on the similarities of that person with you. We all are humans, our needs are similar (food, security, love, happiness, and sense of fulfillment). We all are ignorant at some level and wish to avoid suffering. Next find other areas of similarities. Do you have similar preferences for food? Do you both like to travel? Do you both have unique idiosyncrasies? Do you like similar clothes? Are your movie choices similar? Try to find similarities even in differences. Are you both similar in having unique preferences?

With each in breath, imagine that you are sharing their pain and suffering (known or unknown). With each out breath, imagine sending them healing energy and love. Remember that all six and a half billion of us are biologically related. You just have to walk a few generations up to connect with your neighbor's ancestry tree. Nobody thus is truly a stranger.

Exercise 3. Compassion for someone you are not able to love

Sit in a safe place with your eyes closed. Draw an imaginary circle. Place yourself in that circle. Within that circle, also include someone you are not able to love. This could be someone who may have hurt you in the past, at home, or at work. Try to create positive warm feelings for that person to the extent you can. Do not force yourself.

Now focus on the similarity of that person with you. We all are humans, our needs are similar (food, security, love, happiness, and sense of fulfillment). We all are ignorant at some level and wish to avoid suffering. Is there any other similarity you can find? Are they caring for at least someone, even if that someone does not include you?

With each in breath, imagine you are decreasing their pain and suffering. With each out breath, imagine sending them healing energy and love. If you can, forgive them just for this moment and accept them for what they are. But do not force this feeling. Go only as far as you feel comfortable. Be open to the possibility that you might feel more compassionate toward them tomorrow than you are today.

19. Acceptance (Acceptance for Wednesdays)

Your perceptions depend on the quality of your attention and how you interpret the information you receive. The greater your ingrained bias, the farther your perceptions are likely to be from the truth. Realistically, it is extraordinarily difficult to completely let go of the bias. However, here is what you can do to decrease the negative impact of bias:

- minimize the bias by *being more objective*;
- be willing to consider possibilities that do not align with preconceived notions by *being more flexible*;
- develop a perspective that is closer to the reality of everyday life by *nurturing wisdom to pursue the truth*; and
- develop *willingness* to work with the imperfect, undesirable, or uncontrollable.

Acceptance is a combination of these four aspects: objectivity, flexibility, pursuit of the truth, and willingness. Acceptance entails developing greater equanimity.

What is Acceptance?

Objectivity: Acceptance is your ability to minimize bias. Acceptance is your willingness and ability to see things as they really are and not as you prefer them to be. It is an internal acknowledgement of "what is" as you prepare for the appropriate response. Acceptance entails deepening and sustaining attention, delaying interpretations and their related judgments. This enriches your sensory input providing you more time and thus more details to help you arrive at an interpretation that is closer to the truth.

Flexibility: Acceptance is an inner flexibility in your mind processes. Acceptance allows you to consider novel possibilities that may not necessarily align with your preconceived notions. This willingness offers flexibility to your thought and behavior and is critical to learning and adaptation, and to participate in a team both as a leader as well as a part of the team. **Rigidity, with few exceptions is a sign of ill health while flexibility is a sign of wellness and growth.**

Wisdom and the pursuit of truth: Acceptance is searching for and collecting knowledge that is closer to the truth, irrespective of its desirability. Developing a model of the world and its parts that is closer to how they actually operate is likely to empower you to better describe, predict, and influence phenomenon.

Willingness: Acceptance also is (at least) temporarily becoming comfortable with the imperfect, undesirable or uncontrollable and willingness to engage with it. The purpose is to decrease negative emotional reactivity as you try to improvise, correct or adapt to the disagreeable. This is the "approach" strategy compared to "avoidance" that may disengage you from the world and increase stress and dis-ease.

Research shows that acceptance is sometimes difficult to learn, particularly if you have a predisposition to experience negative mood. This may be partly because acceptance is often confused with apathy. A common question patients and learners often ask me is, *"With acceptance am I resigning myself to fate, becoming apathetic, and not doing what I should be doing?"*

My response is an emphatic No. Apathy is loss of passion and hope and reflects pathological pessimism. Apathy signifies gloom, is almost sinful, and will never lead to the higher goals toward which you strive. Apathy expresses itself as listlessness and is often reflected in expressions such as, "Whatever" or "I just work here." Nothing could be further from acceptance than the feeling of apathy.

Acceptance, on the other hand, represents hope, optimism, and faith. Acceptance is making the snowman each time it snows knowing fully well that it will eventually melt when the Sun shows up. Joy is in the process of making the snowman, not in having it last forever. By becoming comfortable with the reality of imperfections, undesirable and sometimes uncontrollable outcomes, as well as finiteness, acceptance helps remove fear and fosters a deeper engagement with life. Acceptance is maintaining an inner balance so you can cultivate strength that facilitates passionate action. This passion is rooted in calm. It is this combination of passion and calm that promotes creativity and growth of the individual and the society. ***External effort powered by internal acceptance generates a strong and focused action.***

When expectations do not match reality, an internal battle often starts that leads to frustration and anger. **A battle with the self can not be won.** Acceptance allows you to step out of this largely unnecessary battle. This stepping out saves energy, prevents premature reactions, and helps enhance your joy. Further, by letting you see the reality and giving you greater time to respond to the situation, acceptance helps you engineer the response constructively.

A key aspect of acceptance entails recognizing that there is a limit to what you can control. The reality is whether we like it or not, often what is beyond our control is way more than what is fully within control. This realization saves you energy since you focus on the controllable aspects of your life rather than feeling despondent about the uncontrollable components. Acceptance, thus helps create a realistic world model where uncertainty can be more easily accommodated. Once this wisdom is fully understood and embodied, it is immensely empowering because it diminishes your unwillingness to experience unpleasantness. This unwillingness is a significant contributor to our suffering.

A constant practice of acceptance leads one to surrender. Surrender, like acceptance, may sometimes be misunderstood. *Surrender is the ultimate feeling in optimism, a belief that the world is just and fair and that the right long-term path is to follow the principles of fairness and justice.* Surrender also entails cultivating a secure belief that the world cares about you because you are a most intimate and precious part of the creation, just like everyone else is.

Mature surrender is rooted in the deepest wisdom. Surrender recognizes that our contextual knowledge that is limited by our paradigm critically depends on our ignorance. Anything we see depends on clarity of our vision to that point but also inability to see further. This could lead to infinite regression with progressive ability to see a deeper reality. Surrender looks at this exercise with engaged amusement and recognizes its ultimate limitation. The ultimate "why" may be unanswerable because it comes with a load of assumptions that our mind cannot easily reject. Every answer will only sprout a future question. Armed with this wisdom one learns that it is most adaptive to not peg one's peace or joy on the specifics of contextual knowledge. This breeds surrender, an offshoot of the deepest wisdom. Greatest peace may hide in relinquishing the need to know. **Pick blessings, not knowledge, if you are given only one to choose from.**

You are blessed when you are content with just who you are. That's the moment you find yourselves proud owners of everything that can't be bought (Matthew 5:5 MSG).

I realize there are times when acceptance, as it might be understood superficially, just does not seem fair or appropriate. Many of these situations are where innocent, well-meaning people are faced with markedly adverse events in their lives. Optimism and faith may be severely challenged in these times and need significant strength and courage to sustain. A few approaches alone or in combination that might help you turn around the adversity and preserve some sanity include:

- considering disruption as your spiritual stress test;
- trying to find meaning in the adversity;
- considering adversity as a challenge rather than as punishment;
- expanding the world view to include imperfections;
- keeping the faith;
- reading inspirational stories; and
- realizing (and accepting) that there are aspects of life that are just beyond individual control.

Each of these is a step toward developing acceptance.

Inner acceptance is a critical point in your journey from disruption to transformation.

20. A few good reasons for acceptance

Exercise 1. Imagine you have to give an important presentation. Your energy is likely to be distributed in two directions: 1) externally toward preparation for the upcoming presentation; 2) internally toward reflexive generation of anxiety about the process and outcome; attempts to suppress this anxiety; frustration at inability to do so; decreased quality of life for the next two days awaiting the presentation; and once the presentation is over, ruminations on how the whole thing went focusing mostly on the negative (Figure 20.1).

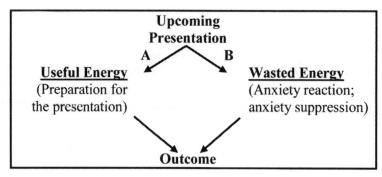

Figure 20.1 Two directions of the flow of your energy

If the energy you use toward preparing for the presentation is depicted as A and for the anxiety reaction and associated phenomenon represented as B, try and rate yourself where you stand.

1. A = 20%; B = 80%   ☐
2. A = 40%; B = 60%   ☐
3. A = 60%; B = 40%   ☐
4. A = 80%; B = 20%   ☐
5. A = 100%; B = 0%   ☐

If you marked 1 or 2, you are in a state of non-acceptance; 4 or 5, you have trained yourself well; 3 is somewhere in between.

Exercise 2. Now ask yourself what parts of the variables in this specific example are in your control (Table 20.1):

	Yes	No
1. Preparation for the presentation	☐	☐
2. Quality of your presentation	☐	☐
3. Mood of the attendees	☐	☐
4. Bias of the attendees	☐	☐
5. Working audio-visual system	☐	☐
6. Outcome of the presentation	☐	☐

Table 20.1 Variables that are or are not in control

There is a good chance you probably marked No for options 3-6. The outcome of your presentation depends on several variables that are beyond your control. If you have no control over any of these, then why sweat over them and drain your energy? The energy you spend in the generation of the anxiety reaction and its downstream effects goes to waste. Often this is the more difficult part to handle than even the original issue at hand.

*It is good to remember that **"some things you desire, some you are willing to accept."*** If you have a flat tire in the middle of the road, you cannot just sit there lamenting on your luck or the source of origin of the errant nail. You accept the situation and engage with it to fix the tire and reach home. If your car's engine light turns on, breaking the light will not fix the problem. It will only mask what lies behind this light potentially exposing you to a greater risk. Acceptance allows you to see what this light truly means and then optimally address it. *A stitch in time saves nine.*

There are four additional reasons why acceptance might be a good idea.

Non-acceptance may keep you in a state of fight with yourself

Who wins if you pick a fight with yourself? Certainly not you. A fight with the self cannot be won. In medicine, some of the most difficult illnesses to treat are those where the body reacts against itself. Cancer and autoimmune diseases are good examples of such conditions. An attempt to neutralize such deviant cells almost always causes collateral damage to the normal cells. Our societal challenges are also similar—external wars are easier to fight; internal wars are the more difficult ones; worst are the wars where officers in the internal ranks themselves mutate into destructive enemies.

In the same vein, battle with an outside ego is much easier compared to a fight with your own mind. If you pick a fight with your own mind, the fight is never likely to end. The fight goes on until one day you realize there was no reason to fight in the first place. You always had the option of not fighting this war but were not tuned to avail it. You can step out any time and make internal peace with the imperfections. Unfortunately, oftentimes this realization comes very late in our journey. Acceptance fosters internal peace early on despite the outside imperfections. Acceptance thus helps you respond more effectively to the outside challenges.

Accepting others as they are is the most efficient approach to bring about a change in them

There is a good chance you are surrounded by people you wish were a bit different. Your spouse or friends probably are not the same as they were when you first met them. Your older parents might be changing and getting more stubborn. Your children may not always behave like the gentle angels you wish them to be. Your employees, colleagues or supervisors may not be as flexible and accommodating as they seemed to be at the first impression. A large part of your energy may be spent in efforts to bring all these "others" to a more desirable state—mostly without success. If any of this applies to you, please be comforted that you are not alone.

Part of your unhappiness certainly comes from the fact that the people around you have imperfections (just as you do). But the greater part of unhappiness comes from your desire to control and change them and frustration at your inability to do so. The more you try to change them, the greater will be your assault on their ego and the less likely they are to change. The one person who predictably listens to you and will be most willing to change at your suggestion is you. Trying to change others is an insurmountable task and one fraught with a high risk of failure or distancing yourself from your loved ones. The most efficient way you can change others is by changing yourself.

The key to open the door for change in others is with them, not you. Only they can open that door, once they are willing. They are likely to be more willing on a day they feel good about themselves. They will also listen to you more openly if they perceive your unconditional warmth toward them. What do you think is the first step to enhance their self esteem and show them your warmth? *Accept them as they are.*

Acceptance allows you to learn from failures and turn them around into success

Life will always bless you with failures. World is not always going to be fair. Inequality is the very basis of creation. The important point is how you tackle your failures to transform them into success. In the midst of planning and taking actions, it might help to internally accept that some of your plans will not materialize and actions will not bear fruit. In fact, sometimes it truly is a blessing that your plans did not materialize. You might only come to know years later what an opportunity it was when something you desperately wanted to achieve eluded you.

Failure is always painful. Failure, however, is much needed and the sooner it happens, the higher you are likely to go. Within failure are hidden the golden lessons to help you learn and grow. In fact, one of the important attributes of many successful entrepreneurs is their early experience of failure. *Ability to turn a failure into opportunity and advancing not only despite failures but sometimes because of failures is a hallmark of resilience.* Resilience is an ability to learn from and grow with each change and challenge. Resilience depends on a healthy and mature strategy toward handling failure. An essential ingredient in this approach is an attitude of acceptance. With acceptance, the more you get disrupted, the greater your learning and the higher you go.

Acceptance helps you engage with the controllable

Exercise 3. Which of the following do you get to choose of your free will (Table 20.2)?

	Yes	No
Parents	☐	☐
Siblings	☐	☐
Country of birth	☐	☐
Race	☐	☐
Your health	☐	☐
Falling in love	☐	☐
Children	☐	☐
Children's health	☐	☐

Table 20.2 Aspects of your life you have little control over

You may have answered "No" to all or most of the above. Even falling in love—because love just happens—may not directly be in your control. These are some of the most important aspects of your life that determine its direction. Realize that your extent of control over the world is limited. It only extends to simple, often trivial things. This holds true no matter how accomplished and influential you are. This realization is not to increase anxiety about uncertainty but to instill a sense of humility. It is the humble equanimity that will allow you to find islands of peace within the ocean of uncertainty that is your life.

So how best to invest your energy? Let us do this next exercise.

21. Organize your challenges

If you like to make lists then you might like this exercise.

Exercise 1. Identify your challenges and categorize them into one of the four quadrants as shown below. Use additional sheets if necessary.

Controllable→ ↓ Important	Controllable	Not so controllable
Important	A	B
Not so important	C	D

The exercise above is particularly helpful if you have a lot going on in your life, which for some of us may be a rule rather than an exception. Now let us develop a systematic approach toward each of the quadrants. I have filled out a few suggestions below.

Controllable → ↓ Important	Controllable	Not so controllable
Important	**A** Take care of the aspects of your life represented here. Relationships occupy this quadrant.	**B** All your past and some of your present and future occupies this quadrant. Learn from it, and bring <u>acceptance</u> and <u>forgiveness</u> to the contents of this quadrant.
Not so important	**C** Think about cost vs benefit. How meaningful is it to you? Learn to let go if the cost significantly exceeds benefit and it is not very meaningful.	**D** Let go of what occupies this quadrant.

You only have a limited quota of energy, physical as well as mental. You would like to allocate your energy to the most significant problems that are amenable to solutions. Purposefully pick the challenges that are worth responding to based on their relevance and your ability to impact them. Otherwise you risk cultivating a reactionary approach, dissipating your energy, and may not be able to optimally focus on the most important things. **Your ability to prioritize the challenges you choose to respond to is very important to decrease your stress.**

Our next steps that guide us deeper into mature acceptance will now elaborate on these very ideas.

22. Acceptance: additional exercises

Exercise 1. Invited or just showed up?

Spend some time in your garden bringing your full presence. Notice all the plants. Did all of the plants, weeds and blades of grass receive your invitation or some just showed up on their own?

1. All received an invitation   ☐
2. Only some received an invitation   ☐

Some of the plants you may have planted….others came of their own volition without your specific invite. Isn't it?

Not every plant or blade of grass growing in your garden had your invite. On any given day your garden has both, the weeds and the flowers. You may, if you like, work extremely hard to get rid of every little weed and unwanted plant from your garden and make your garden perfectly immaculate. But then, that is all you might do all spring! And if your attention wavers even for a day or two, an irate weed might just show up. The process however has another cost. While obsessively clearing all the weeds, you are likely to miss on something precious—enjoying the beautiful flowers that manifest in your garden. These flowers generally do not wait for our attention to complete their journey. They are leased to us by Mother Nature only for a brief period of time.

A more balanced and flexible approach might be to divide your attention between clearing up the weeds and attending to the flowers. Remove as many weeds as you can, particularly the larger more obvious ones, and then accept that maintaining a perfect weed proof lawn is impractical, even undesirable.

When with your loved ones, focus on the blessing of togetherness. Delay judgment. Meet them each time as if you are meeting them after a long time. The first step toward a deeper engagement starts with accepting them as they are. Like the tulips this spring, your time with them is finite and generally shorter than you might imagine or like.

Exercise 2. Did you preplan all the flowers this spring?

Stroll through your garden and notice all the plants, with or without the flowers. Did you know in the winter precisely which plant will blossom how many flowers and in what arrangement?

As you plan your garden, all you can do is to plant the right seeds, provide them the right nourishment, protect them from the elements, and then just wait. Your hurry or impatience will not accelerate the arrival of the sapling. Some of the seeds will oblige, others will wither away. Not all plants that are born from these seeds will find an eventual place in your garden. You are mostly thus an observer, with each plant pursuing its own journey as your co-traveler. **Breaking chrysalis open prematurely does not deliver a happy butterfly.**

You will enjoy your garden more if you do not excessively impose your preferences or bias on Mother Nature and learn to appreciate the flowers that have blossomed, accepting them in their natural beauty and arrangement. It might be better to respect the decision of a plant that chose not to blossom this season and give it some more time. Further, keeping a realistic expectation that some plants will not oblige almost every season and it is often difficult to spot them ahead of time will also help. It is likely that this is how nature assures that with its limited resources, your garden and everyone else's garden has flowers blossoming each spring.

Exercise 3. Wake up to the impermanence

Look at any aspect of your life—home, work, relationships, or even your own emotions. Do you think things are more likely to stay the same or change?

1. Stay the same   ☐

2. Change   ☐

Since the beginning of creation, our world is constantly changing. Change is a way of nature. Getting comfortable with change is an essential step toward inviting peace. Progress almost always entails change; every change, however, is not progress. Change could entail a loss, gain, or transformation. Loss is often the most noticeable and most hurtful change. Loss of what you hold close to your heart is usually a painful experience. It is only natural to love and be attached; these feelings form the very basis of creation.

Love, however, finds its greatest intensity when it is rooted in the acceptance of finiteness. Every moment then becomes unique, special, and precious. Finiteness is the reality. The sun has to set for the stars to twinkle. A flower has to let go of her nectar for her pollen to spread. A flower also has to wither for the fruit to come. The person you dearly love will have to go away some day. You and I will eventually surrender everything we hold dear. Try to see a world where no one ever dies—it is a pretty congested place. Know and absorb the transience of each moment, live it to the full and then let it go. Understand and then accept that you will forever face change, and this change will not always be pleasant or desirable. Your stress and grief come not from the change *per se* but your attachment and desire for perma-nence. The sooner you imbibe the lesson of impermanence, the quicker you will be able to access the state of joy. Do not postpone sharing your love; and do not save your love for only special moments. ***When the time comes, it will be easier to say good bye when you have loved deeply and were able to express it.***

Exercise 4. Track the journey of your life

Go back down the memory lane into your life and start from the beginning of your career (point A) to now (point B). Look at two possible tracks shown below. Model 1 depicts a journey that is straight up; while model 2 shows a more zig-zag course—a few steps forward a few behind.

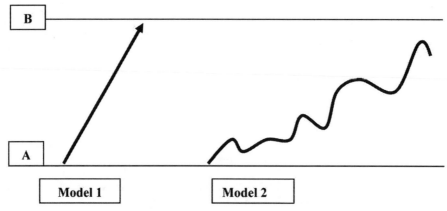

Figure 22.1 The two models of growth

Ask yourself this question:

Which model more accurately depicts your progress so far, model 1 or model 2?

In general, model 2 is a more accurate depiction of our life's journey. For most of us, progress comes in steps that are interspersed with a lull phase or even a step back. The step back prepares us for the next phase of progress. In general, when faced with a period of reversal, it might help to nurture a long-term view, keeping in mind that each of us have our own unique path, that will likely work out over the long haul, as long as we keep the perspective that ***a step back often is a move forward.***

Life is a journey. You spend the bulk of your time traveling. Wherever you reach is a starting point for the next trip. You seldom stop at any of your destinations. Such is the nature of life. The fun part is often not the final stop but the entire journey. If you spend your journey thinking, dreaming, and worrying about the destination, you might spend your entire life never having experienced joy. Our natural instinct is to be just a bit ahead of ourselves. While taking a shower, we often are mentally at the breakfast table and at the breakfast table mentally in our office. With this approach, we may not show up for the bulk of our life. Accepting and engaging with the present moment will enhance our presence.

Gain and loss are the natural chatter ingrained within the overall journey. Accepting this variability and incorporating this into your overall model of life, you can cultivate a state of inner equilibrium that is not likely to be easily disturbed by the frequent stronger gusts and will have better resilience to withstand the occasional severe storms.

Recognize the true nature of life. Most of the time is spent traveling. Your commute is the end in itself. This commute is but a series of present moments stacked upon one another. So enjoy this moment here and now. Be awake as you travel. The best way to live happily ever after is to live it in the now. Attend to the tree, the streets, the shops, every friend waving at you as they pass by. And whenever you can afford to, stop and smell the roses.

Exercise 5. Make peace with the past.

Answer this question about your past. What is the best strategy to approach your past?

1. To observe and learn from it   ☐

2. To spend a lot of time regretting the past   ☐

3. To close your eyes to the past   ☐

You probably chose the first option—to observe and learn from it. Your ability to observe and learn depends on acceptance of the past as it was. If your past was unpleasant, acceptance prevents the imperfections of the past from contaminating the beauty of the present. Just as roasted seeds do not germinate, a past that is accepted may not haunt and annoy you as much. Acceptance of the past stops you from feeding more energy into the negative experiences, thus disempowering the attention black holes that might be lodged in your memory.

Our mind, however, has a great propensity to excessively consult the past before allowing us to be happy in the present. The past draws attention to both happy and unhappy moments, more often the latter. **We tend to judge the past based on what we know today.** Past events, thus might look unacceptably imperfect. The past could have been better or it could have been worse. The fact is it could not have been either. It was what it was because that is what it was meant to be. Be amused by your past without attaching too many judgments to it. Your past contributes to your current emotions; while how you feel in the future will greatly depend on your present experience.

Accept that if you have painful memories they will not completely go away. The kernel of attention black holes will remain buried within layers of newer and fresher memories. If you send energy to these black holes by dwelling excessively on the unhappy events, they will be further empowered, fresh, and hurtful.

Develop a more accepting relationship with these memories by knowing the reality. And the reality is that these memories are like your unpleasant cousin who embarrasses you, causes you grief, won't go away—but is not vile. No point fighting him, just accept him as he is. Include in your worldview the existence of an imperfect cousin. Similarly, make peace with these unhappy memories and accept them for what they are. They cannot harm you anymore, as long as you choose to accept and transcend them. When they do, however, surface once in a while, do not put too much energy suppressing them. Instead observe them in a detached way. Watch your thoughts float by as if you were seeing ducks floating in a stream with you sitting on the bank. The moment you start observing your feelings, you stop owning and identifying with them. The outer layers of rumination and avoidance gradually disappear from your attention black holes. Even the dark kernel in the center may be reinterpreted as you begin to find meaning in your suffering. It is then that you start learning from those memories. These negative feelings thus serve a great purpose by providing you a perfect opportunity for growth.

Exercise 6. Islands of acceptance

Find a time and place where you feel safe and can let go of intentions. Remain in total acceptance of the past, present, and future, with no intention to judge or reason. Let go of the tendency to plan or problem solve. When your mind tends to wander, bring it back to the sensory experience in the present moment, breath, or your daily theme (gratitude, compassion, acceptance, meaning, or forgiveness) to keep your mind anchored. An ideal time to practice this would be at the time of your daily prayer or meditation or during the times you are instructed to train your attention.

See how acceptance of "what is" instills peace and brings bliss to you from your inner self. Prayer brings peace partly because when praying, we are instilled with a feeling of acceptance. We accept the divine presence of our devotion, be it a thought, an image, or a word, with no judgment. However, if you bring an intention of a self-focused reward into the prayer, its beauty and purity will go away. Such a prayer is often not relaxing.

With constant practice of acceptance, you might find yourself more patient, humble, compassionate, gentle, and kind. As you become more comfortable with these ego-free moments, expand them into other periods of your life.

Exercise 7. Island of mindlessness and non-acceptance

We are often not able to sustain our presence in the present moment because of living in a fast-paced world that forces us to multitask. If your responsibilities ask you to take your mind in different directions at the same time, trust me, you are not alone and count me also with you! This is very common with the patients I see since there is so much they have to figure out. In this state, it is easy to slip back into mindless awareness and non-acceptance. Often there is a lot going on in life that needs your attention. In fact, this may be a rule rather than an exception. I find two useful approaches in this situation: keep the perspective; and schedule some times for mindlessness.

By keeping the perspective, I mean being able to keep in mind that most of my fears are not going to come true; my hurry is mostly internal; everything I have is ephemeral and finite; suffering is universal; and a hurtful expression from someone toward me shows that they need help or hug (and not an unkind reaction).

Accepting a time for mindlessness decreases guilt and internal conflict when you have no choice but to be mindless. During your day, you can allow fifteen minutes of time wherein your mind is not held with any leash and can think unrestrained. You could call it your *"worry break" or "scheduled worry time."* In this time, take your mind through all your plans and concerns and let it think what it likes to think. Use this time to address all your fears. Through the day when you find yourself worrying, note down the concern and allocate that concern to this time. If there is a lot you have to resolve, take out thirty minutes or even an hour—whatever you can dispense with and have the need for.

Since you are in acceptance of mindlessness during your "worry break," it might actually become enjoyable. This time may allow you to remain in the present moment the rest of the day. The key is that you be the driver and not allow your mind to feast on your peace. You might experience that, over a period of time, the need for this time will likely fade away.

Exercise 8. Patience

Spend a day in limitless patience. Listen fully and deeply to what others have to say. Eat with patience. Be patient with your child, a forgetful employee or employer, with your spouse or loved one. Try to find wonder in each experience. Select the following choices after such an experience.

Table 22.1 Table for Exercise 8		
	Yes	**No**
Was your day more efficient than usual?	☐	☐
Did you absorb and learn more?	☐	☐
Were you more relaxed than other days?	☐	☐
Did you connect with others more deeply?	☐	☐
Did you feel more fulfilled at the end of the day?	☐	☐
Any other comments:		

The concept of time created by human imagination has enslaved us in many ways. It is interesting that an entity that has no independent existence affects our life so much. Part of this is due to how we relate with time. Time these days is measured in seconds—Internet seconds. Most information gathering occurs primarily by reading the headlines. We tend to react with the speed of an efficient web search engine. We jump to pick up the phone at the first ring, often send an instant reply to an e-mail before having thought through the details. We hear others speak but seldom are truly listening because we already ostensibly seem to know what they might have to say. The window of that momentary pause when they stop to breathe provides us the perfect opportunity to start broadcasting our thoughts! ***All this impatience with few exceptions is purely internal and largely unnecessary.***

Most things will come to you, if only you could wait. Make time for everything you do so you enjoy the process. Speed often is a killer of quality. Forcefully opening a bud will not make the flower bloom. There is nowhere to go once a task is over, just another task. Be with what you are doing and you will begin doing it with greater joy and to a higher perfection. It might take a few more moments. The world can wait and so can you, a few seconds for sure.

Patience is a virtue, often not inherent in us, and has to be cultivated. Practice patience in every day events. At the dining table, while loading the dishwasher, talking to your child, listening to your mom. Just be there at any and all of these times. Look in the eyes of your children as they share the experiences of their benign wonders with you. Try to feel the benevolent voice of your mother. You might find so much wonder and connection that the rest of the world ceases to exist.

Arguments and miscommunication tend to happen because of a lack of our presence, particularly heartful presence. Most people in the world at their core are kind and well-meaning. We, however, project our bias on to what they say. We then fill some of the blanks with our own prejudiced ideas and create an image that is congruent with our thinking at that time. All this might dissolve if you are able to invite patience and trust into each experience and relationship. **Impatience and heartfulness are mutually exclusive of each other.**

To conclude our discussion of acceptance, it might help to summarize some of the lessons we learned in the exercises above. I will state them as individual pearls. The activity is in the form of an exercise. Please pause after you read each point and contemplate it for a moment. Once you feel you have understood the concept, check mark it and then move to the next pearl. If you are not clear, please go back and read the relevant text. You can also use these points when you teach some of these ideas to others.

Table 22.2 Summary of Acceptance		
Pearl #1	You may consult the past to understand the present and anticipate the future, but do not drive looking into the rearview mirror all the time. Accept what has transpired, learn from it, and move on. Make peace with the past.	☐
Pearl #2	What you see as a weed might actually be a flower. It all depends on how you are looking.	☐
Pearl #3	Your source of stress and joy are the same. If you wish away stressors, you might be wishing away your life. Look at a stressor as an opportunity.	☐
Pearl #4	Your circle of control is small. Learn to let go of trivial differences and accept people as they are. This is the best way to change them.	☐
Pearl #5	What is right about you generally trumps what might be wrong about you.	☐
Pearl #6	Impermanence is the truth of life. Everything is in a flux. The sooner you recognize and accept this reality, the earlier you are likely to find peace and progress in life.	☐
Pearl #7	Sharing your blessings is immensely pleasing and is the ultimate treasure you save for your later years.	☐
Pearl #8	Hurry is mostly internal, not external.	☐
Pearl #9	Love, acceptance, and surrender cannot be separated from each other. You love in surrender and surrender in love.	☐
Pearl #10	Carefully pick your battles in life; fix the fixable making sure that treatment is not worse than the disease; let go of and accept the non-controllable by modifying your worldview to also include some imperfections.	☐
Pearl #11	A step back may actually be a move forward.	☐
Pearl #12	A past that is accepted and used to learn useful lessons may stop being as hurtful.	☐
Pearl #13	It is okay to be mindless if you have to be…just be aware that you are mindless.	☐
Pearl #14	Some things you desire….some you may just have to accept.	☐

23. Meaning & Purpose (Meaningful Thursdays)

Meaning in life generally refers to the value and purpose of one's life, important life goals, and for some, spirituality. Another way of looking at meaning refers to the nature of an individual's relationship and understanding of the self and the world. Meaning could span from trying to understand the world at its most expansive cosmic level to the smallest unit of existence at the quantum level. For the present, our focus is somewhere in between, at the level of the individual.

At the individual level there are two aspects of meaning:

1) Our beliefs and understanding of the world (others, circumstances, events, etc.); and
2) Our beliefs and understanding about the self (and our life).

Both these meanings converge toward the single ultimate meaning, which is the present moment. **Ultimately what is most important at this very moment is what you are doing right now. The person most important at this moment is the one you are with right now.**

Recognize that in the tangible world nothing has an independent and complete meaning. All our meanings are contextual. What is the comparative meaning (value) of a $20 bill for someone whose net worth runs in billions of dollars compared to a hungry orphan child who could buy months worth of food with the same money? A telephone operator at the other end of the phone may be just a voice for you, but to someone else she is the precious sweetheart, a mom, a sister, a daughter. She is the epicenter of many little worlds that depend on her. Most birds in your backyard probably have two mouths waiting in the nest. **Everyone means a lot to someone.** It is just a chance that you may not be aware of their larger meaning because you are not that someone (and thus lack the full context). *But you can easily imagine yourself to be that someone.* Once you learn to look at others with the eyes of the person for whom they mean a lot—compassion, acceptance and love will automatically flow. It is a beautiful way to live.

The meaning you carry is extremely important in deciding what you do and how you feel each day. You develop this meaning over a lifetime based on what you see, perceive and imbibe, and how you think. A large proportion of this evaluation, particularly thinking may happen in your subconscious—below your level of awareness. An unrealistically negative evaluation is likely to provide you a biased view of the world and the self that can be very damaging in the long term. Many insensitive acts of physical and emotional violence occur within the milieu of lack of an integrated positive meaning. On the contrary, your belief that this world is just and fair, and that you are ethical, capable, and competent, is likely to improve your self-esteem, efficiency, sense of well-being and physical health, and help you pursue a path toward excellence, even greatness.

Long-term vs. Short-term Meaning

In general, most people carry two different types of meaning:

1) Long-term meaning – this is the global meaning that implies your long-term beliefs, values, and purpose/goals of life.
2) Short-term meaning – this is the situational meaning that is applicable to short-term events.

Once you pause and reflect, you may articulate an eloquent long-term meaning and purpose to your life. The key question is whether your short-term actions and meaning are aligned with this long-term meaning. If the two are strangers, then you are likely to perceive stress.

Short-term or situational meaning tends to be more labile and depends on changing circumstances such as relationships, health, finances, etc. You are likely to be happier if the short-term meaning of your actions is overall congruent with your long-term meaning. A lack of congruence between the situational and global meanings tends to create conflicts. For example, the simple experience of missing an exit on a highway might create a conflict and be a source of stress. This is because your goal of reaching a place is thwarted by the short-term setback of missing the exit. Resolution of this conflict can be achieved by either changing the situational meaning or the global meaning. It is easier and more efficient to reappraise the situational meaning. In this example, you may not want to change the goal of trying to reach your destination, even if a bit late. However, for the short term it might help to consider that had you not missed the exit you may have never noticed the interesting bookstore right around the corner or got an opportunity to spend some more time with your daughter.

Meaning is a fundamental dimension of an individual and depends on a multitude of variables that affect a person's life. These could be social, cultural, religious, philosophical, and personal values. Search for meaning is an important component of several psychological theories that describe how individuals adjust and prevail in their situation. It is by finding meaning that individuals have climbed the heights of greatness. Meaning transformed their work and responsibilities into their prayer and calling.

24. The three types of meaning

The three types of meaning reflect the close emotional ties you develop; the most important goals you wish to achieve in the physical world; and your concept of spirituality. In general, across the life span, your beliefs about the world and self can be adapted to three fundamental aspects of your lives:

 a) belonging (relationships);
 b) doing (work or leisure activities); and
 c) understanding oneself and the world (spirituality)

Pause for a second and appreciate that these three aspects—relationships, work and leisure, and spirituality capture most of what you do and experience in your life. It is within these three domains that we shall further develop the concept of meaning.

A. Meaning by Belonging

Relationships provide an identity, a sense of self to us. A question I often ask of patients I see in the clinic is: What provides meaning to your life? The most common answer is—family, mostly children or spouse. My next question then is: What is the source of your stress? The answer again is—family, mostly children or spouse. **Our fountain of meaning, love, and also of stress often starts at the very same source—our relationships.**

Relationships are our life blood, the primary source of our joy. You may then wonder why our loved ones become the primary source of our stress. *An important reason for this is that we do not interact with our loved ones on a day-to-day (short-term) basis the way we deeply feel about them.* Our short-term and long-term meanings are then not aligned. We also take their presence in our life for granted and remain oblivious to the meaning they provide to us. As a result, we fall short in our relationships. Love however multiplies best when it is shared.

Exercise 1. In the exercise below write the five closest relationships that define you as an individual. For example, I am a wife, I am a father, I am a friend, etc.

I am a _____

I am a _____

I am a _____

I am a _____

I am a _____

What you wrote above represents your primary source of joy—your inner circle. This is your oasis and cushion that nourishes and shields you on a daily basis. Later, we will discuss how best to sustain and enrich this inner circle so you can thrive (and not barely survive) in it.

Beyond this inner circle, there is also an important outer circle that can also be a source of great joy and sustenance. In order to be optimally effective and happy, you need a healthy relationship with both the circles, inner and outer. The outer circle includes people in your community, your town, your country, our planet. The larger the circle you draw, the more members there are in your family. As your awareness unfolds, the inner and outer circles converge, the distinctions become blurred. It is when you feel connected with your "larger family" that you can share your joy and in turn, be nurtured by it. It is this connection that fills your heart with compassion, even for strangers.

B. Meaning by Doing

There are only a few things you can do day after day, week after week, month after month for years together. One of them is work. Most vacations, fun expeditions, and other leisure activities if overextended will likely eventually lose their charm. Beyond the material needs to pay your bills, work provides a sense of self-worth and meaning to your existence. This may be particularly so if your work provides an optimal change and challenge, there is opportunity to grow, you get a fair compensation, expectations are predictable, you have a sense of control, and are accorded due respect.

Work is healing because it provides a sense of self-efficacy. Work provides you a broader perspective and a sense of control since you can make things happen. This becomes even more important when you voluntarily or involuntarily have to leave your work—an issue that will be faced by the seventy-seven million baby boomers as they begin their retirement years starting 2011. The sum total of research suggests that loss of meaningful work has negative effects on health.

In research studies, retirement has not been found to be associated with increase in sports or non-sports leisure-time physical activity and may be associated with weight gain, particularly in women. Such effects, however, have considerable individual variability that is related to how you choose to spend your retirement time and are able to put energy behind your choices.

So how best can you make the golden years really golden? The most important aspect is to develop a sense of meaning and purpose for this phase of life. Keeping a disciplined schedule and engaging in meaningful activities wherein people or project/s depend on your attention and care will help your-self esteem, keep you healthier, and might even increase your longevity. Such meaningful work does not have to be structured or limited to a specific definition of how the work is understood. Continued engagement in any purposeful activity that provides you a sense of self-worth may obviate many of the negative effects of inactivity that comes with retirement. This is particularly so if you approach it with energy. Research shows that if you provide support to someone else, you are likely to remain healthier for a longer time.

A kind person is doing himself a favor….(Proverbs 11:17 ICB)

You could look at what you do as a chore that you have to complete to pay the bills. *On the other hand, you could consider your work as a calling* and approach it with a drive and passion that allows you to transform your micro world in a small yet precious way. The latter approach is likely to drive away stressful feelings that sometimes come with work. People who look at their work as their calling become the agents of change. Intellect is not in short supply in this world; what we need is focus that is energized by enthusiasm. Attaching your work with something larger than you may provide it a higher meaning and is likely to help you cultivate that enthusiasm.

Sometimes, however, the full meaning of what you are doing may not be easily discernible, particularly in a large and complex organization. In such instances, a belief in the existence of a larger meaning and maintaining a state of joyous acceptance while being absorbed in the activities of the present moment will likely bridge the time until the meaning spontaneously unfolds. **The continuity and thread of our purpose is often apparent only when we look back.**

C. Meaning by Understanding Oneself and the World (Spirituality)

Spirituality broadly relates to a combination of faith and meaning (meaning through faith). Spirituality is believed by some to provide a transcendental meaning to life, a sense of knowing that sometimes cannot be fully expressed in words. What is considered spiritual is very individual. For some, spirituality connotes one's relation with nature, for others it is work, family or community, and for still others spirituality means a relationship with God or even a metaphysical or transcendental phenomena.

Religion and spirituality are closely related. Religion can simply be understood as an individualized instruction manual of living. Religion represents beliefs, practices, values, and rituals that help people fulfill their spiritual needs. Many religions are associated with recognition of a higher power commonly understood as God or another exalted being.

Let us explore next some of the ways we can enhance our ability to find a higher meaning in what we do.

25. Finding higher meaning

We can search for a higher meaning in our life in the three core domains: relationships, spirituality and work. I will discuss aspects of relationships in chapters 29 and 30. We will focus here on spirituality and work.

Spirituality Could Provide Meaning for Believers and Non-believers Alike

Spirituality has a broad definition that includes one's relationship with nature, work, family, community, God, and metaphysical / transcendental phenomena. Finding meaning with any of the above could be considered spiritual. By that token, many people who consider themselves atheists might actually be deeply spiritual.

Exercise 1. Try to understand your personal spirituality by answering the next three questions:

Q1. Do you consider yourself a spiritual person? Yes / No

Q2. If yes, in what aspects of your life are you spiritual? (Check all that apply)

Relationship with nature ☐

Attitude toward work ☐

Attitude toward family ☐

Attitude toward society ☐

Faith in God ☐

Belief in metaphysical ☐

Others_____ ☐

Q3. Write how you plan to deepen your spirituality

In your relationship with nature

_____

_____

In your attitude toward work

_____

_____

In your attitude toward family

_____

_____

In your attitude toward society

_____

_____

In your faith in God

_____

_____

Others

_____

_____

There is a very good chance that you care about several issues noted in question 2 of this exercise. You are thus spiritual in your own unique way. However, sometimes this inner spirituality may not find an easy venue for expression. This exercise is to remind and help you discover your essential spiritual nature and find greater meaning in it.

Finding meaning in work

Exercise 2. How do you see your work? Check only one option (Figure 25.1).

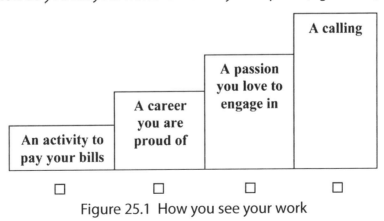

Figure 25.1 How you see your work

Recognize that the higher level includes the earlier ones. Thus, if you consider your work as your passion, it will still be your career and pay your bills. However, work that is your passion will provide you greater meaning.

Let us see if we can find higher meaning in what we do.

Exercise 3. In the exercise below try to fill out the three most important work-related roles that you accomplish every day. For example—I am a teacher; I am a homemaker, etc.

I am a _____

I am a _____

I am a _____

Now ponder for a moment and try to find a larger meaning in what you do. For example, if you are a teacher, you provide the education and mentorship to the next generation of professionals so they can go out, succeed, help others, and further the cause of your country.

Exercise 4. In a few words describe how your work helps you, your family, community, and country.

My work helps me by –

_____

_____

My work helps my family by –

_____

_____

My work helps my community by –

_____

_____

My work helps my country by –

_____

_____

What you wrote above is the larger meaning of what you do. On a not so lucky day when you are feeling low for any number of reasons (particularly related to work), it might help to remember the larger role you fulfill. This might prop you up a little and provide you the needed energy to continue your pursuits with enthusiasm.

Now for the final exercise in meaning:

Exercise 4. What would you do differently (that you are not doing presently) with your loved ones, spirituality, work, and in other aspects of your life (e.g. leisure) if you were told that you have only a short time (a few days) left to live?

With loved ones

_____

_____

Spirituality

_____

_____

Work

_____

_____

Other aspects

_____

_____

Your answer to this exercise informs you about your priorities and how you really feel about your loved ones and others. The chances are, with little time left, you might spend more time sharing your love, care, and kindness. In the midst of an event that threatens one's survival, no one wishes to look at their 401k account statement. One of the most important thing one wishes to do in this situation is to call their loved ones to say goodbye and how much you love them. If this is how you deeply feel about them, why not live with these feelings most of the time?

It might also be a good idea to address all the things you identified you would like to do if you were to have a finite amount of time left. There is a good chance that if you take care of these urgencies, it will take a load off your chest and give you a sense of freedom. The fact is that we all have a finite amount of time, we just do not think about it. This realization should not be a reason to become depressed; on the contrary, it should prompt you to live each moment to the fullest.

We are almost coming to the weekend now! We covered Gratitude for Monday, Compassion for Tuesday, Acceptance for Wednesday, and Meaning and Purpose for Thursday. As the next step now, we will discuss Forgiveness, our theme for Friday.

26. Forgiveness for Fridays: basic concepts

In the last two decades of my interactions with the patients and learners, the three most common questions I have been asked about forgiveness are:

- "If I forgive, am I not passively justifying the wrong done to me?"
- "How is forgiveness linked with my current health condition?"
- "Does an inability to forgive contribute to my stress?"

My answers to these questions are:

- Forgiveness does not mean you have to justify the wrong done to you. You may choose to forgive irrespective of whether someone does / does not deserve it. You forgive because you choose to live a higher, more fulfilling life. You forgive because you are and want to become emotionally and spiritually more mature.
- Lack of forgiveness is intimately related to many of your medical conditions. Research studies show that by practicing forgiveness, you are likely to be healthier and happier.
- Lack of forgiveness is a drain on your energy and prevents you from engaging with the beautiful present. Lack of forgiveness gets you stuck in the past and definitely contributes to stress-related symptoms.

You might be misinterpreting forgiveness if you think by practicing forgiveness you will have to necessarily justify, excuse, or deny the wrong. This misinterpretation often leads to a feeling that forgiveness isn't fair, particularly if you harbor significant anger or resentment. Thus, forgiveness is not any of these:

- Justifying;
- Excusing;
- Condoning; or
- Denying the wrong

Forgiveness does not prevent you from taking all the appropriate measures for your future safety, or even pursue a legal recourse if you have to. Forgiveness does not usurp any of your basic rights.

Forgiveness, on the other hand, is a choice that you make to cultivate emotional maturity and lead a more spiritual life. **Forgiveness is for you, not for the forgiven. Forgiveness is a voluntary choice that you make to give up the anger and resentment despite knowing and accepting that the misconduct happened.**

Forgiveness is your gift to others that often comes to the undeserving. Further, by practicing forgiveness you become kind to yourself. *Forgiveness is your spiritual stress test.* **You can see your ability to truly internally forgive as a tangible milestone in your spiritual journey.**

Let us develop a good understanding of forgiveness with the following exercise.

Exercise 1. Develop a good understanding of forgiveness (Table 26.1)

Evaluate these statements and make a judgment as to which ones you agree with.

Statement	Yes	No
Forgiveness is a gift from me to others	☐	☐
I am not obligated to forgive, forgiveness is my willful choice	☐	☐
My forgiveness is often directed to the undeserving	☐	☐
By forgiveness, I do not intend to forget the wrong	☐	☐
By forgiveness, I do not intend to deny the wrong	☐	☐
By forgiveness, I do not intend to justify the wrong	☐	☐
By forgiveness, I do not intend to allow people to get away with or repeat the misconduct	☐	☐
I can stop the process of forgiveness at any point I become uncomfortable with it	☐	☐

Table 26.1 Understanding forgiveness

All the correct responses in this exercise are "yes."

Do you see that forgiveness is really for you and has the potential to help you *without* necessarily usurping any of your preferences or rights?

Forgiveness, however, isn't an easy skill to learn and practice. In fact, forgiveness can be mentally challenging and stressful and, particularly when the hurt is fresh, seem totally unacceptable in the short-term.

Exercise 2. Read through this list that compiles the benefits of forgiveness and check those reasons with which you agree.

Table 26.2 Table for Exercise 2	
Forgiveness does not mean you justify, accept, excuse, condone, or deny the wrong	☐
Forgiveness means you choose a higher, more mature form of living	☐
Lack of forgiveness is stressful	☐
Lack of forgiveness with related anger might hurt your health	☐
Lack of forgiveness generally serves no tangible material purpose	☐
Lack of forgiveness keeps you stuck in the past and may prevent you from a deeper engagement with the present moment	☐
Lack of forgiveness drains energy	☐
Forgiveness improves several health outcomes	☐
Forgiveness helps decrease anger	☐
Forgiveness is a moral good	☐
Forgiveness frees up the mind to focus on the future	☐
Forgiveness improves relationships	☐
You are forgiven, likely several times, every single day	☐
Forgiveness engages the higher centers in your brain	☐
Eventually all of us will have to forgive and / or forget	☐
Every scripture you revere preaches the virtue of forgiveness	☐
Most of the greatest persons you admire, practiced and taught forgiveness	☐

27. Forgiveness pearls

I wish to share a few pearls that are mostly based on the results of research studies with forgiveness. Some of the pearls are also based on what appeals to basic common sense and are a part of everyday experience of yours and mine. The ideas presented will form the basis of a few forgiveness exercises that follow in the next chapter.

Pearl #1. Consider forgiveness a lifelong process

Forgiveness is a process that progresses at its own natural, generally slow pace. Trying to attain "quick fix" forgiveness is unlikely to work. Be deliberate and patient and try not to hurry yourself into forgiveness. This is particularly true for deeper hurts. When hurt in a bad way, particularly when the injury is fresh, recognize that it may be difficult or impossible for you to immediately consider forgiving the wrongdoer.

Pearl #2. It is okay to be selfish in forgiveness

Particularly, for the more egregious transgression, it takes almost super-human effort to cultivate warm and charitable feelings. It is thus okay to start by focusing on the self. I call this *altruistic selfishness*. You forgive because you wish to heal, stop your pain, and disempower the person who has hurt you. In the process, you may reach a point of equanimity where you are able to let go of the past and eventually start wishing well for the transgressor. This often happens simultaneously with your perspective becoming more global, where you begin to focus on essential humanness of everyone including the wrongdoer. Such a perspective is likely to percolate into other aspects of your life, bringing with it the priceless gifts of peace, joy, and freedom.

Pearl #3. Broaden your world view to include imperfections

In the eyes of a child who has never seen pain or misery, this world is nothing but a place to explore, play, and have fun. It will, however, help you to keep a broader worldview wherein, unfortunately, evil also has a place. There are people in this world that choose the path of being evil. Bad things happen even to innocent and good people. If you have ever been injured, you know that evil is real and only a breath or a thought away. Incorporating a broader worldview that includes the existence of evil might allow you to better deal with the challenges of life and thereby, find a more secure peace.

Lack of kindness often happens in moments when we lose self control. It may be out of anger, greed or even self defense. Sometimes, we innocently hurt the very people we love the most. Keep a low threshold to forgive in such situations. We all are bound to commit mistakes. ***You do not punish the teeth that may have innocently bit your tongue.***

Pearl #4. Try to understand others' actions

Most of your thoughts and actions can be interpreted in multiple ways. There is a good chance that none of us are either right or wrong all the time. As you mature and expand your zone of acceptance, many behaviors that might have otherwise appeared wrong may start seeming appropriate. This is because you start seeing everyone's point of view. Most behaviors and actions have a reason behind them. An ability to understand the specific reason rather than prematurely using and adding to your prejudices might help you in the path toward forgiveness. In this context, it will be helpful to look at human beings as fallible and limited. Often, you might find yourself at a loss as to what you would have done if you were stuck in the same situation. Remember that, *"An expression other than love is often a call for help."* The vast majority of people who seem angry or frustrated are stuck in their own attention black holes. They are fighting their personal inner battles. The purpose is not to justify but to understand. Refuse to accept the gift of their anger. Research studies show that it is easier to forgive others if you see yourself capable of committing a similar offense.

Pearl #5. Consider forgiveness as an opportunity

It will help if you ask yourself this question: On the whole, has lack of forgiveness helped me or hurt me so far? If you think lack of forgiveness has not helped you and you are willing to consider the alternative, take this as an opportunity to grow rather than something that would hamper your progress. This might help propel you toward emotional and spiritual resilience. You do not have to deny the existence of negative memories. The kernel of these memories will persist. However, you can stop sending more energy toward it and prevent it from becoming an attention black hole. Accepting the negative memory by including a worldview that includes imperfections helps you make peace with it. You may find this strategy opening new doors to help you grow.

Pearl #6. Exercise the privilege to forgive as soon as you recognize the need for it

Try not to serve the stale food of unforgiveness of previous hurt as the main course of thoughts the next day. Especially for minor offences, do not let the sun set and rise again with unresolved hurts and resulting lack of forgiveness. Short-term anger directed against a wrongdoer may be appropriate and sometimes even is needed. However, in general the longer you ruminate about a hurt, the stronger its roots, which makes it more difficult for you to forgive. Look deep within and try to surface the feeling of forgiveness as quickly as you recognize the need for it. This is particularly true for minor grievances. However, if this feeling simply cannot be found in this moment, then don't force it. It won't work. As long as you nurture the intention to forgive, the chances are that the freshness of tomorrow morning might take you there.

Pearl #7. Forgive gracefully without creating a burden on the forgiven

Think about a time when you may have hurt someone (deliberately or by mistake). You may have felt guilty and vulnerable in that state. You likely still feel embarrassed about your actions and would rather not be reminded of the event too many times. The same holds true for others. Reminding people repeatedly that you have forgiven them will likely make them defensive and resentful. The best approach is to not create any incremental burden or challenge for the forgiven. *He that giveth, let him do it with simplicity (Romans 12:8 KJV).* Let forgiveness not be used to show your magnanimity or virtuosity, to appease someone or, worse, to advertise how others have been wrong. Bring genuine compassion into your forgiveness.

Pearl #8. Forgive before others seek your forgiveness

Waiting for someone to ask for forgiveness might turn out to be a very long wait. It will only delay the moment at which you can freely begin to embrace your own destiny. Studies show that children often need an apology to be able to forgive. But as a mature adult you can choose to transcend that need. It takes tremendous courage and humility for anyone to accept they were wrong. The whole life sometimes goes by trying to muster that courage. Admitting a mistake is a sign of courage but is curiously considered a sign of weakness in our society. It is fair to assume that many people do not have the emotional resources to stand up and accept their guilt unconditionally and so will not easily ask for forgiveness. Remember what we discussed earlier—forgiveness is for you, not for them.

Pearl #9. Look forward to forgiving

Do not consider forgiveness a burden, a heavy chore, or something that might take energy away from you. The truth, in fact, is the opposite. In the long run, forgiveness saves you energy. So look forward to forgiving. In fact, consider forgiveness a privilege. Often the wrong that happened may have created new and unique benefits. In this context, research studies suggest that writing about potential benefits of a negative event might allow easier forgiveness.

Pearl #10. Extend your forgiveness toward what might even transpire in the future

Your ability to forgive the past is an important milestone in your journey toward happiness. As a next step, what might immunize you from future suffering will be your ability to forgive the future. Forgiving the future entails accepting your loved ones as they are right now as well as accepting them how they will be in the future. This is the greatest gift you can give them out of your compassion and love. I prefer to call it "Pre-emptive forgiveness" and regularly teach this to learners who are ready to practice it. This is particularly helpful for minor irritations within the folds of trust and love. If you can truly internally forgive and accept future annoyances that might come your way, you have in effect inoculated yourself and others against much future suffering. This does not mean you will allow indiscretions. All it means is that you will be in control of your own emotions and not allow anyone else to evoke anger or resentment within you.

Pearl #11. Praying for others increases your ability to forgive them

Research studies show that if you pray for the other person (friend or loved one) you are more likely to develop a forgiving disposition toward them. So in the context of a loving relationship praying for each other might make pre-emptive forgiveness easier to embody.

Pearl #12. Prevent future situations where you may have a need to forgive

We tend to create expectations of the way this world should reward us. Often we do not share this expectation with anyone, certainly not in clear terms. Instead, our pride gets in the way—subconsciously we remain fearful that our insecure ego will be bruised if we express our desires and they are not met. Ego thus hides these desires. Despite hiding our desires, however, we carry a hope and a subtle expectation that these desires will still be fulfilled. We might even feel entitled that they eventually are fulfilled. The foregoing is a storm brewing. If you keep unexpressed lofty expectations, you might be creating a setup for disappointments and hurts. The three-part solution to prevent this from happening is:

- Lower your expectations;
- Clearly communicate these expectations; and
- Keep an attitude of internal acceptance that you will not be surprised or disappointed if these expectations are not met

Pearl #13: Lower your expectations

Having lower expectations strongly correlates with experiencing greater happiness. This balances the E-R equation (expectation-reality) and is likely to lower your disappointments. For example, Denmark often ranks at or near the top of the list of the happiest places on earth based on interviews with natives of different places. A survey titled "Why the Danes are Smug" was conducted by the University of Southern Denmark in 2008. Results showed that the main reason for people's happiness is their low expectations. Low expectations avert disappointments and also prevent creation of situations wherein one might find a need to forgive.

Pearl #14: Have a low threshold to seek forgiveness

Forgiveness is not just about forgiving someone. *It will also help to keep an appropriately low threshold for seeking forgiveness from others if you think it is reasonable and might help.* Research studies show that when one is emotionally hurt, they are likely to experience significantly unhealthy heart rhythm and that once you express an apology, their condition remarkably improves. So if your loved one is hurt for any reason, do not leave them with an unhealthy heart beat. Seek forgiveness sooner rather than later.

28. A few forgiveness exercises

Forgiveness is sometimes a difficult, painful and slow process particularly for the deeper hurts. If you have ever been hurt, please know that it is just fine if you are presently unable to forgive. I fully respect and understand your predicament. Forgiveness is one of the most difficult challenges you may have undertaken, particularly for the more serious hurts. So be kind to yourself. Engage the help of someone you trust, including if need be a professional. Do not try to fast track it. Let it unfold at its natural pace.

I am providing a few exercises here that I thought may be of help. I fully realize they can in no way replace the well meaning and supportive tribe around you that is so important in helping your path toward healing.

Exercise 1. Have you ever desired to be forgiven?

Think about a time when you may have hurt someone's feelings. Now answer these questions in a fair and objective fashion (Table 28.1) .

Statement	Yes	No
Did you intend to hurt their feelings?	☐	☐
If you knew your actions would hurt their feelings would you have done the same thing?	☐	☐
Does your action make you all bad?	☐	☐
Would you appreciate being forgiven?	☐	☐
Do you wish to apologize but are not able to muster enough courage at this point?	☐	☐
Would you feel relieved if they came up to you and said in a kind, friendly way they have forgiven you?	☐	☐

Table 28.1 Your experience with forgiveness

In all probability:

- You did not intend to hurt
- You would like to be forgiven

- You wish to apologize but are not able to collect enough courage to do so (maybe you are too embarrassed or even shy)
- You would feel relieved if you knew they have recovered and moved on

It is possible that the person who wronged you may have hurt you unintentionally, is currently repenting, but is not able to come forward and apologize. *"Do unto others as you would have them do unto you."* (Luke 6:31)   Forgive others as you would want them to forgive you.

Exercise 2. View the person / event in context

Often the event or experience is evaluated by us based on its immediate short-term personal value. Consider this scenario.

Jon, an overworked sales agent, finds it irritating that he gets the most difficult clients to work with. He is particularly upset one day because his current supervisor, Tim, always picks on him and gives him the extra work. Jon holds a grudge against Tim, considers him unreasonable, and is not particularly kind when he fills out Tim's evaluation. A few weeks later Jon receives a commendation letter from the CEO of his company along with an unexpected bonus. It turned out that Tim gave Jon the most difficult clients because he thought Jon was the best. It was Tim who recommended Jon for the bonus. Jon is happy and embarrassed at the same time.

Applying the scenario to your situation, consider the totality of circumstances. Do you think the person who hurt you purposefully intended to harm you? Was s/he fearful or stressed when s/he acted? Is s/he perhaps also suffering (e.g. from childhood abuse, work related issues, etc.)?

Now try and answer these questions:

Table 28.2 Table for Exercise 2		Yes	No	Don't know
Statement		**Yes**	**No**	**Don't know**
Is it possible that the reason you were hurt could be different from what you are thinking?		☐	☐	☐
Is it possible that the person who wronged you could have acted –	with incomplete knowledge of the facts	☐	☐	☐
	in a state of confusion	☐	☐	☐
	when stressed	☐	☐	☐
	in self-defense	☐	☐	☐
Is it possible that the anger was misdirected at you?		☐	☐	☐

None of these may be correct in your specific situation, but considering one of these possibilities has the potential to decrease your stress and begin your journey toward forgiveness. It might help to assess the totality of the situation that led to the event rather than primarily focusing on the immediate action of the perpetrator.

Exercise 3. Find meaning in suffering

Forgiveness is particularly difficult when we feel we have been willfully harmed. It is easier to forgive if we can find some meaning in suffering. Almost every negative event has a potential opportunity. Many of the healthy and ethical things in life are not entirely pleasant or easy in the short-run (think about adhering to daily exercise or a low calorie diet). If you wish to progress, it is important to focus on the long-term and see what lessons you can learn from the negative experience.

Write on a piece of paper any possible way that your suffering or the person who hurt you, may have actually indirectly (perhaps unknowingly) helped you.

- Is it possible that the wrong done to you may have prevented something worse that could have happened?

- Could your hurt be a wake-up call to help you work toward greater physical, mental, and spiritual resilience?

In the table below complete the two columns for your specific situation in the spirit of the suggested examples:

Table 28.3 Table for Exercise 3

The stressor	Assigning meaning
I got fired from the job	I learned new skills and found a better position
She won't let me smoke inside the house	She is helping me quit
He was mean and tested my faith	He helped strengthen my faith

Exercise 4. Find meaning in the process of forgiveness

It will be much easier to transcend your hurts if you can assign meaning to the process of forgiveness. *See if you agree with the following statements and add a few of your thoughts to the text box below.*

I will be able to focus my mind better if I am able to forgive
Forgiveness will allow me to strengthen my faith
By forgiving, I will be able to share a more pleasant attitude with my children
By forgiving, I will become more resilient and have better self esteem

Exercise 5. Cultivate acceptance and empathy

Once you decide to consider forgiveness, it might help to generate acceptance and empathy for the wrongdoer. This process will be helped if you:

- Minimize ruminations on the wrong that happened;
- Try and find similarity between you and the other person; and
- Try to see the good in the other person

Based on these feelings try to accept others as they are. Each one of us is unique, incomplete, and imperfect in our own way. *That is why we are Homo sapiens not Homo divine.* Every landscape, every garden has imperfections. Acceptance of these imperfections might help you enjoy the beauty that is inherent in all of us.

Write three good things (if you can) about the wrongdoer:

1.
2.
3.

Try to use some of the exercises described in the chapter on compassion (chapter 18). Recognize however that developing compassion for the person who has hurt you may be enormously challenging and should not be forced. This process may be greatly helped by keeping a broader, all-encompassing view of the world. In this view, you recognize the imperfections, and try to find a place for the wrong doers. Having a spiritual role model also helps with this and all the other previous exercises.

I will now introduce you to some of the supportive exercises toward forgiveness.

Exercise 6. Forgiveness imagery, first exercise

On a peaceful sunny day, watch a distant cloud in the sky. Collect all your hurts and park them on that cloud. See the cloud gradually float away, taking all your hurts with it. Practice deep, relaxed breathing with this exercise.

Exercise 7. Forgiveness imagery, second exercise

Collect all that you have to forgive in a folder. Realize that it is too heavy and toxic for you to keep. Forward this folder to the power you define as the creative intelligence running this planet. Let that intelligence deal with it as s/he considers appropriate. At your end, consider the job done.

Exercise 8. Release your emotions, first exercise

Write a letter to the person you intend to forgive. Put all the details about the event and state clearly why you were hurt. End the letter with a few lines specifically addressing your intention to forgive. Read this letter as if it has already been received by the person. Then shred the letter.

Exercise 9. Release your emotions, second exercise

When you are on a beach, write your grievances on the sand close to the shore and watch the waves wash the words away. Keep that imagery in mind so you can relive this experience later. This will help you consolidate the benefits. Practice relaxed deep breathing with this exercise.

Exercise 10. A day of forgiveness

If it is not easy to forgive just yet, it might help to create an island of forgiveness, a day or even an hour at a time.

Live a day of your life having forgiven everyone. Try to practice this at least once a week (Fridays are the assigned days of forgiveness in our program). Say to yourself several times that day, "Today I am in bliss. My ability to forgive makes me feel healthy and happy. I carry no grudges and feel compassionate toward everyone. Whatever happened is buried in the past. I forgive, for I have been forgiven many times." If a day is too long, practice forgiveness for just an hour.

It might help to commit to someone close to you about this exercise. This will make you externally accountable and better able to comply. If the memory of the hurt comes to you that day, postpone ruminations about it. Assign yourself to think those thoughts the next day. The joy of forgiveness might help you expand this time (from an hour to a day, to a week, and further on).

Exercise 11. Meditation on forgiveness

Take slow, deep, diaphragmatic breaths. Imagine that with each exhalation you are releasing out all your hurts, injuries, and negative feelings from your heart. Imagine that with each inhalation you are imbibing positive energy and forgiveness of the universe into your heart. In the beginning, practice this meditation for five to ten minutes every day sitting in a safe and quiet place. You can increase the duration of the practice as you advance.

Remember these beautiful and true words: To err is human, to forgive divine (Alexander Pope). Forgiveness raises you from being a human to the state of being divine and awakened with a life transformed.

Exercise 12. Pray for forgiveness

If you find it difficult to forgive today, do not hasten the process or force it upon yourself. Just pray that you get the strength to be able to forgive and stay with that prayer for some time. Tomorrow or day after, you will find greater strength and ability to forgive.

Now for a very important and final exercise in forgiveness:

Exercise 13. Pre-emptive forgiveness

I conducted a simple yet transforming experiment in the beginning of 2008. As a new year resolution, to a close loved one I promised unconditional forgiveness for the entire year of 2008. I resolved that everything they say or do, I will take in a positive light. This commitment enhanced our quality of life tremendously. It took away any little disagreements, judgments, miscommunications and all the other annoyances that do not deserve to, but sometimes come in the way of fulfilling relationships. The wonderful aspect of this experiment was that later I received the same commitment from them also and we have been renewing it yearly.

Learning from my own experience and from sharing it with others, I highly recommend pre-emptive forgiveness within the context of a close loving and trusting relationship. Most minor disagreements are not worth paying attention to. If a year is too long, may be start with one day. Start your journey into pre-emptive forgiveness by praying for your loved ones. Research suggests that if you pray for your friend or spouse, it will be easier for you to forgive them.

I often tell patients and learners to just live the day today in full preemptive forgiveness. At the end of the day see if you carry a smaller burden on your shoulders. This is the perfect vaccination against much future suffering. Preemptive forgiveness does not mean you will allow indiscretions. All it means is that you will be kind to yourself, in better control of your emotions, delay judgment, do not allow amygdala to hyper-react, and train your brain to be more heartful so your brain's higher center instinctively comes on line. *This could be potentially transformative, particularly if you add to preemptive forgiveness also preemptive acceptance.*

Your forgiveness for yesterday may heal a sore that knows not its healing balm; your gift of forgiveness for tomorrow may heal a wound yet uncreated, yet as hurtful as the one experienced. *If you consider forgiveness as a gift, remember that gifts are often given for the joy of the present and the future. So gift preemptive forgiveness to your loved ones. You are, thus gifting them and yourself the promise of a life with much greater joy.*

29. Your tribe

Pause for a few seconds and think about something extraordinary that you have desired all your life. It could be winning a lottery, having a child, marrying your boyfriend or girlfriend, getting a raise, or anything else that you hold very high in value…Now imagine a day in the future when this desire actually is fulfilled…

Exercise 1. How many friends and relatives would you call to inform about your good fortune knowing they will be truly happy and proud when they hear about your accomplishment and not expect you to share any part of it?

1. None ☐
2. One ☐
3. Two ☐
4. Three ☐
5. Four or more ☐

These friends and relatives constitute your tribe. Consider yourself extraordinarily lucky if you have a few friends and relatives who will truly rejoice in your success. **It is easier to share sorrow; the true test of friendship is the ability to share joy.**

Your own tribe is made of friends and relatives that share some of these characteristics:

1. They accept you as you are
2. They know you are imperfect and are okay with it
3. They understand you
4. They desire nothing but the best for you
5. There is an aspect of you they admire
6. They are honest with you
7. They consider your success theirs; your suffering theirs
8. You consider their success yours; their suffering yours

There is a good chance you are surrounded by people who share these characteristics but may not have paid attention. In addition to the question asked above, an answer to the following question might also help.

Exercise 2. Who among your friends and relatives can you call at two A.M. in the morning without a concern they will be upset or judgmental?

They constitute your tribe!

Exercise 3. Based on this understanding identify the first five members of your tribe.

1. _____

2. _____

3. _____

4. _____

5. _____

Let us now introspect how we relate with the members of our tribe.

Positivity:Negativity (P/N) ratio (Gottman)

Positivity is the positive feedback you provide to others while negativity is the negative feedback. Within a team, a P/N ratio of five or above suggests excellent team dynamics while low performance teams often have a ratio below one. Marriages that flourish often have a high ratio (typically >5) while those that might end up in divorce have a low ratio (often <1).

Exercise 3. Estimate your positivity/negativity (P/N) ratios for your five closest relationships. For this exercise we will use the following definitions:

P/N ratio for feedbacks: (P/N^f)

> Positivity = Number of positive feedbacks

> Negativity = Number of negative feedbacks

P/N ratio for kind actions: (P/N^k)

> Positivity = Number of kind actions

> Negativity = Number of disciplining actions

Both of these are to be estimated in the previous three months and include a range of 0 to 10. Score 0 = when you provided no positive feedback and did no acts of kindness. Score 10 = when you provided 10 such feedbacks or actions for each negative one. If your score is >10, please mark 10 for the purpose of this exercise.

Name of the person	P/N^f ratio for feedbacks	P/N^k ratio for kind actions
1		
2		
3		
4		
5		

Guilty as charged!! There is a good chance that you have many loving relationships but may not have made efforts to keep a high P/N ratio. Relationships are likely to get strained if you do not keep a healthy P/N ratio. Remember that some of us are better at kind words and others are more doers. Give your loved ones some leeway if they are not able to excel in both these aspects.

Exercise 4. Based on what you learned above, if you wish to redeem yourself (assuming you have the need to do so, which I believe most of us do), in this exercise write one kind thing (words and/or actions) you will do to show your appreciation of your loved ones. It does not have to be elaborate or expensive and could be as simple as an unexpected phone call or an e-mail showing you remembered and cared about them. Remember, it is the little every day things that count the most.

#1_____

      Planned kind words   _____

      Planned kind actions _____

#2_____

      Planned kind words   _____

      Planned kind actions _____

#3_____

      Planned kind words   _____

      Planned kind actions _____

#4 _____

      Planned kind words _____

      Planned kind actions _____

#5 _____

      Planned kind words _____

      Planned kind actions _____

Let us now focus on a few additional ideas to create and sustain your tribe.

30. Creating and sustaining your tribe

Creating a tribe is a bit similar to taking care of your garden. The three key steps in creating a garden are: seed it, feed it, and weed it. First you do the appropriate landscaping, take care of the soil, sow the appropriate seeds, and plant the right plants (your friends and loved ones). All this while feed your garden with water, a rich soil and fertilizers (your presence and love). You consistently maintain your garden and remain patient that one day the seeds will germinate; saplings will grow and bear flowers and fruits. You need lots of patience to let the process unfold at its natural pace; a prematurely opened bud does not deliver a happy flower. Once the garden shows the colors of green, pink and purple, to keep it pristine, you also have to regularly weed it (of miscommunications, disagreements, hurts etc.). In this entire process, the creation and sustenance of your tribe depends on one person central to your tribe—you.

Seed Your Tribe

Tribes do not get created spontaneously. Creating and nurturing your tribe will be the work of a lifetime. You will need to seed the tribe with a lot of "you." As a first step, you will have to include yourself in your tribe. This may sound counterintuitive but is true. You are indeed the most important member of your tribe. If you are not "present," you might find yourself distant from everyone and everything you hold dear, even while in their physical proximity.

If you do not actively engage, your tribe stands the risk of slowly withering away. Be aware of your "presence" or lack thereof. **When hearing, truly listen. When looking, truly see.**

Kindness may be effortful, until it becomes effortless. Particularly kindness to the self. It is important for you to be kind to yourself and have a healthy self-esteem. Your connection to yourself is the first and most critical step toward finding an anchor for you to creatively create and sustain your tribe.

We will focus rest of this chapter on sustaining your tribe.

Use Kind Language

Language is a living being. Quite often, however, the words may belie the emotions veiled beneath them, particularly in the ambiance of formality. If you remain attuned to the emotions that hide behind the words, you may be able to respond in a much better way to the core issue at hand. Sensing the emotions expressed by others needs your presence and your ability to process the words in the context of other non-verbal messages.

If your loved ones choose irrational words, do not automatically react to what is spoken. Try to understand their inner feelings. *An expression other than love is often a call for help.* Maybe they had a tough day and the only reason they are irrational with you is because they trust and love you more than anyone else in the world. If you take a broad enough view, their irritation toward you may in fact be flattering. By negatively reacting to their words, you might miss the whole point.

Use the language of your heart. You can always find the right words to speak untruth yet not be literally wrong. This is not the way friendships get nurtured. If you choose ambiguous words to dodge the truth, those words might often reflect a compromise. Such words cannot be the language of your heart. Words have intrinsic energy and should be carefully chosen to be a kind reflection of your inner thought process. Be sincere in your compliments. If you are not sincere when you praise, you will likely not believe the compliments that come your way.

I once heard someone say, "A compliment a day keeps the counselor away!"

Find Meaning in an Argument

Volcanoes, angry as they are, still serve an essential function. Volcanoes release pressure from the bosom of the earth and serve a purpose—that of preventing an earthquake. Look at this value in each argument—sometimes it is your arguments that keep you together. What separates us often connects us.

When in an argument, remember that the particular point of contention is almost never more important than your relationship. Details of the events and their interpretations tend to be fluid. You might be looking at some of the aspects with a myopic eye. It will be kind to give others a benefit of doubt. Never let relationships sour because of trivial events. Whenever possible do not accumulate small, low-grade irritations. **Do not let leaky faucets annoy you—get them fixed in time.**

In an argument, do not globalize the issue. Use kind language that you can later own. By globalizing a small issue and using unkind language, you are likely to increase the damage and rev up your limbic system and that of your loved one or friend. To prevent an argument take a broad look. Many things that do not make sense might seem more appropriate once you take a look at the total picture.

Try to understand others before expecting them to understand you. See details from others' vantage point—it might make a bit more sense. Consider their limitations and fears. Assume they are trying to defend themselves and not harm you.

Using these guiding principles, you may be more likely to create space for together-ness. Your boundaries will then loosen, you will be able to create a common center of gravity and not remain in your own cocoon.

If You Ever Get Critical

This is a very important issue. Be very discreet yet leave some room for uncertainty in your critique—in peace or within the scope of an argument. Also use language that focuses more on you than the other person. For example, if the coffee you are served is cold, it might be better to state something like, "I find the coffee a bit cold for my taste." You are likely to receive an accommodative response with this state-ment. If, however, you say, "You always serve coffee colder than it should be," what do you think you will hear? Go make your own coffee! You asked for it because you pinned down the other person in a corner and attacked his or her ego. *If you cannot be polite, be at least vague!*

Critique often reflects the past and not how things might shape up in the future. So it is ideal to focus on the future, not so much on the past, except to draw lessons from it. In the coffee example it might be even better to say, "Mostly I prefer coffee a bit warmer than what it was today. If we could warm it up a bit more in the future, it might help." You certainly used more words but shifted the focus to the future where the person hearing the comment feels capable of making a change. A cri-tique should address the issue in the kindest words and then point toward how the issue can be addressed. This is how you redirect the energy of the recipient toward a tangible solution rather than the fact that he or she was critiqued.

I also suggest following a one-minute rule. When you have to criticize some-one, particularly in their absence, do it for only one minute. Following the one minute rule might prevent you from globalizing the issue and adding extra layers of your own biases. At the end of the day you will likely feel better about yourself if you confined to facts rather than exaggerating and bad mouthing the other person.

Timing of the critique is also important. How we feel about ourselves varies from one day to the next. Accordingly, we may be more accepting of the critique at par-ticular times or days. Try to reserve potentially unpleasant feedbacks to times when you perceive the other person is more open and receptive. We all have moments when we are more open to receive critique. **Right words at the right time are a gift; right words at the wrong time can create a rift.** *To everything there is a sea-son…. a time to keep silence, and a time to speak. (Ecclesiastes 3:1, 7 KJV)*

There is an old Sufi teaching that the words we speak must pass through three gates (introspections): Is it truth? Is it kind? Is it necessary? Only thoughts that pass through these three gates should be spoken, particularly when providing a critique. *Sometimes it is better to speak silence than speak words.*

When You have to say No

It is important for you to pick the size of the bite that you can easily swallow. A bigger bite is challenging to chew and could potentially be risky. In order to right size the bites of your life, you sometimes will have to say No, even within your tribe. The time when you say No is one of the most delicate and vulnerable times, even within a close relationship. If not handled with great care, your "No" can significantly risk your relationships. Let me present an example.

You are asked by your spouse to share lunchtime on a work day. You, however, are behind and would rather work through lunch. Your response could be, "Sorry, I am too busy. Can't come today." An alternate albeit longer response might be, "I would love to share the lunch time, but presently I am facing several deadlines that I have to meet. I cherish our time together and would like it to be fun and relaxed rather than hurried, so how about next Monday during lunch?" Which response do you think would you like to hear?

When someone asks a favor of you, they are put in a vulnerable spot and should be handled very, very tenderly. It is your job to cushion them at that point. Even if you have no choice but to say No, in most situations the first response should be a show of enthusiasm for their suggestion (as long as you truly feel that way). Next you can honestly and in adequate details explain why you are not able to accept their proposal. As a third step, offer the second best option that at least partly compensates for what they asked of you (assuming that is reasonable).

Do you see that your No is guarded by a Yes on both the sides? That is your polite and considerate No. A No that respects the other person. The sequence is Yes-No-Yes. This is the *sandwiched No*. Like it or not, to preserve sanity you will face many occasions when you have no choice but to say No. Use No gingerly, plan how to say it, and know when to say No. This will keep your tribe healthy.

Flexible in Preferences

If within your tribe you constantly worry about how others might be judging you, you are not with them—you are only with yourself, in your head. You are either excessively self-conscious or self-absorbed. Effective communication is not possible in this state. Relationships offer the ideal ground to practice your presence and share higher values of gratitude, compassion, acceptance, forgiveness, kindness, and love.

Make every effort to enhance peace in your circle. One of the ways you can invite peace in your circle is by being easygoing. **Be flexible in your preferences.** Learn to enjoy watching others enjoy. Try to understand, delay judgment and assume innocence. Keep the principle of assuming innocence unless proven guilty. Do not fill the blanks with negative thoughts. Either leave them blank or try to find the best possible explanation. You are more likely to be right (and happier) with this approach. Whenever possible go with the flow. If you find someone wrong from your perspective, consider the possibility that they might know something that you do not.

Kind Words or Kind Actions?

We all have travelled a long and precious journey that is unique to us. Conditioned by this journey our individual needs are also unique. Some of us are thrilled to hear honest praise, may be this is something we missed as a child. Others really love to receive gifts, diamonds in particular! Some others appreciate any help they can get with household chores. Many others want just quality time. Some simply love chocolate! Would it not help for you to know what are the needs that your loved ones really want fulfilled?

Recognize the human nature to do even more of what we can do well. Our propensity is to overfill and over satisfy a particular need—the one we feel most capable of accomplishing. Often your loved one may be giving a different message. Listen to that message because it is a valuable feedback. If you try to fill a part of them that is totally empty, that will offer an excellent return on your investment! If you are not clear which one to choose (kind words or kind actions), start off with quality time. Try it, for I have never seen adding quality time to a relationship not help!

Be Kind to the Self

Kindness to the others starts from kindness to the self. Being kind to yourself is an important ingredient that greatly helps your presence. Kindness to the others radiates from you once you are kind to yourself. Such kindness provides the glue that holds your tribe together.

Once a patient of mine said, "The way I treat myself, if I treated everyone else, I would have no friends left." You are your most important customer. On days of acceptance, be accepting of your self; on days of compassion, be compassionate to the self. Your self kindness is the first step toward bringing kindness to your loved ones and friends.

Cultivate Awareness of Interconnectedness

Every morning when you wake up, watch TV, use your cell phone, and sip your morning coffee, millions of people across the world have worked together to make this happen. You may not perceive this connection because you cannot easily palpate it. The fact is every being on our planet is connected with you.

The world is as small or big as you make of it. Your world could include just you, which is likely to lead you into a lonely, self-focused, and unhappy existence. Or your definition of self could be much broader, making you a patient, compassionate, and interconnected being with a reason to celebrate each day.

This world is like your own physical body; every part is connected with, and profoundly affects, the rest. You share the air, water, food, and all the other gifts of your world with everyone else. Perceive this connection. There are greater similarities between you and others than there are differences.

If I look at your and my liver cells in the microscope, I will not be able to tell whether they belong to you, me or someone else. When these cells join together to create an organ such as a heart, liver, kidneys, or brain they still carry no meaning of religion, race, or nationality. When these organs develop together into a new body as a newborn, we come as an innocent human. As a newborn, we cannot even tell ourselves separate from the rest of the world. It is only with the genesis of the mind and the ego that separations begin to appear that isolate us. Go back a few generations and we all come from the same family. Our similarities thus go far back in time compared to our differences. The essence of interconnectedness is to "remember" our common origins and anchor our awareness in that sharing.

In that sense, the universe is truly your extended self and all the more precious. If you wish to preserve your precious world, include as many beings as possible in your circle. Accept them as they are. The bigger the circle you draw, the larger your tribe. **Draw bigger circles.**

We have travelled together quite a bit already on our journey together. I hope it has been worthwhile and enjoyable for you. Next we will learn a few basic concepts related to a personal relaxation program as we conclude the section on interpretations.

31. Relaxation programs

Exercise 1. Do you have a planned relaxation program that you practice on most days?

1. Yes   ☐
2. No   ☐

Exercise 2. If you answered yes, what does this plan comprise of?

1. Playing with children   ☐
2. Reading a novel   ☐
3. Going on a walk   ☐
4. Talking to friends   ☐
5. Playing music   ☐
6. Art   ☐
7. Other hobby   ☐
8. Prayer   ☐
9. Meditation   ☐
10. Yoga   ☐
11. Muscle relaxation   ☐
12. Tai chi   ☐
13. Qi gong   ☐
14. Relaxation tape   ☐
15. Deep breathing   ☐
16. Biofeedback   ☐

Try to practice at least two or more of the above approaches for daily relaxation. My personal favorite self practices are meditation and prayer. Pick a program however that resonates best with you. The three most important aspects of a relaxation program to make it work for you are:

1) Your belief that the program will help you;
2) The philosophy of the program agrees with your view of the world; and
3) You have the time and ability to practice the program.

Select the program you like and believe is feasible for you, and stay with it over the long term. Most scientific studies show that the results are quite similar with any of these programs.

Most programs will not work right away. Every skill you have acquired, whether it is swimming, cooking, or riding a bicycle, takes time to learn and master. The same is true for a relaxation program. It is important to spend some time with a program before making a switch. You have to dig a well deep enough to fill it with water (or oil).

Consistency of practice is as important as the total duration of time devoted to a program. On a busy day, even five minutes of relaxation might be rejuvenating. Ideally, however, a minimum of fifteen minutes every day would be appropriate, preferably up to thirty minutes. One of the most effective relaxations is prayer, particularly a prayer that emanates from the heart.

A heart's prayer

Faith is often expressed in the form of prayer. Prayer is your attempt to connect and communicate with your image of the divine. Prayer is wisdom and love expressed in selfless surrender. Prayer may be simply an act of love or could have tangible goals such as seeking help or success. The first form of prayer comes from the core of your heart; the second form of prayer is that of the mind. *Prayer of the mind seeks for the mind; prayer of the heart seeks for the heart.*

Prayer mixed with ego leads to fanaticism while prayer mixed with devotion generates love. A prayer that has no goals and is a pure expression of love is a form of communication between a child and his/her father (or mother). Such prayer puts you in a state of acceptance, breeds no fear and allows surrender. A pure feeling and expression of surrender is the deepest form of meditation possible. This surrender finds strength in these words: *And remember, I am with you always, to the end of the age (Matthew 28:20).* While praying with total surrender, the devotee, divine, and devotion all gel into a continuum. This is the prayer of the heart. Pray with your heart. **Pray with your heart even if you have to pray for the mind.**

Prayer provides all the benefits of meditation. Prayer from your heart takes you to the fountain of love. This love leads to wisdom. The process of meditation often starts with wisdom. This wisdom then shows you the path of love. Prayer and meditation thus meet each other at the same point.

32. Your garden has flowers....as well as weeds

In this final exercise we will develop a perspective toward the totality of life.

Exercise: Consider the totality of your life—material, physical, relationships, emotional, and spiritual. What percentage of your life globally is right vs. wrong?

1. Right _____%

2. Wrong _____%

There is a good chance that for almost all of you, what is right is greater than what is wrong.

Our reality:

1. Right   90 %

2. Wrong   10 %

How we tend to live:

1. Right   10 to 20 %

2. Wrong   80 to 90 %

As long as there is life, as long as we are breathing, what is right is more than what is wrong. However, we often live life perceiving just the opposite. Why not accept the right that is right and savor it. Recognize that excessive focus on the wrong is a biologically driven instinct that frequently prevents us from enjoying the glory of the present moment.

Do not let the unpleasant conceal everything else that is blessed. Life is a precious opportunity to practice goodness and experience joy. Your sad thoughts tell you that you have experienced pleasure. You can tell darkness because you have seen the light. However, our moments of blessedness, which all but fill our Garden of Eden, sometimes do not register. We move past them unconsciously and wake up only in moments wherein we are challenged. We, thus, might feel more stressed and unhappy than we should be, based on the reality of our life.

Do not allow your feelings of anxiety or stress to overwhelm all the goodness show-ered upon you. Instead of feeling that you are living a life absorbed in stress, try to look at your stress as a detached observer. As an impartial third person, you are more likely to be objective and accurate in your assessment.

Every moment you are in the present and not focusing on pain or misery is a moment of bliss. Do not allow your feelings of anxiety or stress to overwhelm all the goodness showered upon you. Instead of feeling that you are living a life fully absorbed in stress, look at your stress as a detached observer. As an impartial third person, you are more likely to be objective and accurate in your assessment.

Not every plant or blade of grass growing in your garden had your invitation. On any given day your garden has both, the weeds and the flowers. The weeds in your garden sometimes are a creation of your own bias. They are just plants trying to find a safe haven in this competitive world. Maybe they are not as pretty, maybe they have more thorns. The fact is that the more you focus on looking for weeds, the more weeds you will be able to find. Sometimes you might even confuse a flowering plant for a weed.

On a bright and sunny day of your life, you may be amazed to see how all the weeds suddenly disappear. The flowers appear in full bloom and even what seemed like weeds the other day blossom as beautiful flowers. Sun decidedly helps, but the larger part is the state of your own mind. Your garden all but remains the same. The important thing is—where are you looking?

Section IV: Self-actualization

33. Self-actualization

I pray the journey we have walked together provides you a path away from stress toward a state of peace, joy and resilience. The final goal of this journey is self-actualization. *Self-actualized is a person who has achieved the highest level s/he is capable of. Such a person has fully realized his/her potential.* Our goal is to not only provide a path toward stress management and enhanced resilience, but toward self-actualization.

The first step in that transformation is for you to log back on to your life. You do this by training the 3Ds of your attention—direction, duration, and depth. You take control and at least initially purposefully direct your attention away from the mind into the world. You realize you are not your thoughts and can thus direct them at your will. As a second step, you disengage from your prejudiced interpretations. You cultivate wisdom that guides you away from ignorance with its related siblings of cravings, aversions, and excessive ego. This wisdom helps you understand the power of gratitude, compassion, acceptance, forgiveness, and meaning and purpose. Embodying these values disempowers your attention black holes and allows you to focus beyond the self and include the whole. You rob suffering of its continuity. Your interpretations are guided by the principles-based skills and values, and altruistic preferences. The process limits your desires, reduces your expectations bringing them closer to reality, and broadens the diameter of your existence. It is to this wisdom I have appealed with the intention of awakening it.

Armed with this wisdom, you can free yourself from the shackles of predominant self focus. Once free from excessive focus on the self, your cravings diminish, acceptance finds a ground, and judgments, bias, and fears begin to fade. This allows you to refine your interpretations, use them less often, and increase the purity and depth of your attention. The attribute of attention flexibility pulls you away from the mind into the world. In the world, you pay greater attention to novelty instead of pleasure or threat. Once out of your mind into the world and with refined interpretations, your mind automatically clears of the negative thoughts and memories (attention black holes), just as the water mixed with dirt left still on the table becomes clear in the morning. With most of the attention black holes cleared, you feel progressively lighter and freer.

You recognize that the present moment is not a means to an end—it is the end in itself. You know that real and unreal are mere definitions. Beginning and end do not have tangible time points; they repeat and are just representative of an exchange of energy that has been happening and will continue to happen for a very long time. Often this reality is not perceived because of the constant change we experience in our mind. A firm anchor in the present moment allows you to look at the substrate behind the existence and see the unreality of duality. You begin to see how noumenon (the way it is) and phenomenon (the way it seems) are connected. The co-existence of complexity and emptiness is a source of great amusement to the awakened.

At the level of the brain, this process helps re-establish a higher order control of the deep limbic system. The amygdala becomes quiet while the pre-frontal cortex awakens. You are more often task positive than in the default mode. Brain becomes more heartful.

Once your brain's higher center awakens you are able to look beyond the confines of the existing paradigm. You get beyond the influence of the limited instincts and prejudices of the mind and the intellect. With better regulation of fear, the mind becomes anchored in the non-judgmental present, no longer needing to generate excessive or negative thoughts. You march away from ignorance toward wisdom and ultimately toward transformation. As your brain trains and mind awakens, observation leads to direct knowledge and realization; there is no need for interpretation. You do not seek a path toward peace, peace itself becomes the path.

You start seeking the true gain in your life. A true gain is one that cannot be lost. You realize that every material gain you will have to surrender one day—be it your health, youth, vigor, loved ones, even your dear life. You do not barter spiritual gain for any of these. You do not shortchange yourself. You look at each of your material endowments as your tools to progress on the path toward transformation—a gain that is permanent.

As you progress along this path, you might experience higher states of awareness that go beyond the paradigm of science. You access and stay with your essence bereft of the numerous titles and layers of thoughts that accumulate in your life. This is your ipseity, your core unchangeable self. Let us call it consciousness. Consciousness is the most refined form of self-awareness that is effortlessly anchored in the present moment. Consciousness, however, hides if the lake of the mind remains dirty with excessive thoughts. Consciousness exists beyond the paradigm of time and duality, always in the "now." The deeper spiritual connotation of consciousness equates it with a higher, super, or cosmic consciousness (Buddha or Christ consciousness). This is the spiritually awakened state where you become fully aware of the reality. This is the state of total surrender that takes away all the ignorance. You become aware of how the separation of thoughts and energy into the knower and knowable creates the sense of I, me or mine in what is essentially one mass of consciousness. The seeds may seem different but they all come from the same tree.

The unfolding consciousness finds sustenance in such a trained brain, engaged heart and realized mind that leads you into unconditional gratitude, compassion, acceptance, forgiveness, kindness, humility, patience, and devotion toward all. You fully become what you are capable of. An essential aspect of teachings in many faiths is that the potential for this transformation exists within all of us but is covered by the dust of hatred, anger, desire, greed, envy, and fear.

You realize that ego will finally dissolve and your physical being will surrender to nature. There is no doubt that you will face a time when time will finally come to a halt, when past, present, and future merge into the stillness of a single moment. Everything you hold dear you will have to surrender. There are two ways you can allow the ego to dissolve. In the first path, you let nature take its course from the outside. This path for many is riddled with significant suffering. The other way is to dissolve the ego from the inside by cultivating wisdom and love. This path offers possibility of abiding peace and immense joy. I have attempted to map one possible path for you to dissolve your ego from the inside by developing wisdom and love. It is through *training your brain, engaging your heart and thus transforming your life.*

Once you launch onto this path there is no looking back. You progress and no longer remain ego-, family- or ethno-centric; you become world-centric. This is the transformed awakened life. This is self-realization. This is the self-actualized, enlightened you.

Appendix I: Daily Program

The following summarizes a structured program you can follow to embody the concepts discussed above in your daily life. The program addresses skills in attention & interpretations.

1. Training Attention

1. <u>Joyful Attention</u>: Delay Judgment; Pay attention to Novelty
 * Pick four to eight preferred times to pay attention as suggested for 15-20 minutes each. Rest of the day deepen attention as suggested.
 <u>Suggested morning idea</u> – Think of five things you could be grateful for; bring attention to the breath for five breaths; give your body a gentle stretch; feel the carpet beneath your feet; pay attention to your surroundings; pay attention to your sensory experiences (e.g. shower).
 <u>Suggested day time idea</u> – Spend 15-20 minutes with nature
 <u>Suggested evening idea</u> – Meet your family / friends as if you are meeting them after a "long time"

2. <u>Kind Attention</u>: Attend with CALF (compassion, acceptance, love, forgiveness) (I wish you well / The Bless you exercise – to the first 20 people you see everyday)

Helpful thoughts during the attention exercise: For the next 15 minutes -

- **I have nowhere to go, nothing to accomplish**
- **I have nothing to plan, no problem to solve**
- **I just have to "be" with what is in front of me**
- **Where I am is my entire universe**

2. Training Interpretations

Decrease Prejudices; Interpret with higher principles: Gratitude; Compassion; Acceptance; Higher Meaning and purpose; Forgiveness		

Monday	Gratitude		
Tuesday	Compassion		
Wednesday	Acceptance		
Thursday	Higher Meaning		
Friday	Forgiveness		
Saturday	Celebration		
Sunday	Reflection / Prayer		

You can use one of the two approaches to train yourself in this program:

Option 1 - Implement both the components of the program from day one i.e. Trained Attention (Joyful Attention & Kind Attention) / and Trained Interpretations (Daily application of the higher principles)

This option will work best if you:

- Are fully comfortable with the concepts discussed; and
- Are enthusiastic about applying them to your life

Option 2 - Implement the components one at a time.

This option will work best if you:

- Feel the suggested practice seems overwhelming and might further crowd your day; and/or
- You find the ideas interesting but are still not sure

One suggested schedule for option 2 is:

	Kind Attention	**Joyful Attention**	**Trained Interpretations**
Week 1	*Kind Attention (to at least 20 people every day)*		
Week 2	Continue with Kind Attention	*Add Joyful Attention at least two times a day*	
Week 3	Continue with Kind Attention	Add Joyful Attention *four or more* times a day	
Week 4	Continue with Kind Attention	Continue Joyful Attention four or more times a day	*Add Trained Interpretations (Daily application of the higher principles)*

Irrespective of the option you choose, as you practice you will develop your own ideas about how to embody the higher values in your daily life.

How will you know the program is working for you? You might notice in a few weeks a decrease in ruminations, a bit lighter and more peaceful disposition, greater clarity of the mind, and less fatigue and stress at the end of the day. In some instances, sleep improves and participants experience a welcome sense of well-being. You may find yourself more patient, have greater predictability, become more tolerant to uncertainty, are more comfortable with imperfections in others, and with a relative lack of control. You may find yourself humming or singing more often, and feel a sense of freedom. These are all welcome changes and signal that your attention is stabilizing.

At this point (usually after about 4 weeks of enthusiastic practice), I commonly recommend adding a 15-30 minutes practice of sitting meditation or prayer. I highly recommend you to keep deep breathing as a part of this practice. Two such programs are described in *Appendix III*.

A few general tips:

If possible, take a few days off to have better control over your schedule as you start the program. Keeping a partner who will walk along with you tremendously helps. Setting reminders (post it notes, outlook calendar reminders, refrigerator magnets etc.) might help. Remembering to train your attention is often more difficult than the actual practice.

It is important to be kind to yourself all along. Do not overdo it or chastise yourself for missing the practice. A daily diary (*Appendix III*) might help keep you on track. As you cultivate this practice, please make sure you get adequate sleep and take a healthy diet. Both of these are important to develop new neural connections in the brain.

Appendix II – Train Your Brain Engage Your Heart Transform Your Life: Tools and Tips

This appendix offers a broad summary of the skills discussed throughout the book and also offers structure of a program you could follow to bring these skills to your life. Summarized below are the essential elements of what I have shared previously. *We will first look at the overall theme, then the specific practices and finally look at some helpful details.*

Overall Theme:
Tool #1: Training Attention: Attention training has two components –

1. Joyful Attention: Savor the world by delaying judgment and paying attention to novelty. Several specific approaches related to this skill are described in chapter 12.
2. Kind (Saintly) Attention: Look at the world with CALF (Compassion, Acceptance, Love and Forgiveness). (The Bless you exercise)

Tool #2: Refining Interpretations: Refining interpretations has three components –

1. Decrease prejudices and be open for a fresh perspective
2. Give yourself a break (actually many breaks) from the constant planning and/ or problem solving tendency of the mind.
3. Enhance your focus on gratitude, compassion, acceptance, higher meaning, and forgiveness.

Tips for Daily Practice:
Tool #1: Training Attention:

1. Joyful Attention:

    1.1. Pick four to eight preferred times to practice joyful attention for 15-20 minutes each. Some of the suggested times this could be practiced are:

    - Waking up
    - Breakfast
    - Meeting
    - Lunch
    - Presentation
    - Exercise
    - Play

- At the airport
- Shopping
- Party
- Arriving home
- Dinner
- Bed time
- Other times based on your individual life style

1.2. The five specific approaches to practice joyful attention described in Chapter 12 are: Pay attention to novelty; use one sensory system at a time; find one new detail; anchor on to movement; and contemplate on the story.

1.3. Rest of the day (when not actively practicing joyful attention) try to deepen attention by delaying judgment just a little bit more than what you might otherwise do.

1.4. Joyful Attention Score – You can add the number of times you were able to practice joyful attention. This is your joyful attention score for the day.

2. Kind (Saintly) Attention: Attend with CALF several times during the day.

2.3. A simple way to practice CALF is to send a silent "Bless you" to people you meet (friends and strangers alike), particularly the first time you see them during the day.

2.4. CALF score – You can add the number of times you were able to practice CALF. This is your CALF score for the day. Since it is sometimes not easy to calculate a precise CALF score for each day, an approximate score (such as greater than 10 or 20) would suffice.

Tool #2: Refining Interpretations:

An effective strategy to incorporate higher principles in your life is to focus on one daily theme. A suggested schedule that we follow is noted below (also described in Chapter 16):

Monday:	Gratitude
Tuesday:	Compassion
Wednesday:	Acceptance
Thursday:	Higher Meaning
Friday:	Forgiveness
Saturday:	Celebration
Sunday:	Reflection / Prayer

This theme is flexible. For example, if you prefer you can choose to focus primarily on gratitude on Friday or any other skills that are discussed. Having a structure helps provide a particular focus for each day. The purpose is not to exclude other values. You will realize with practice that each of these values converge toward one core value—that of love.

Helpful Details:

Here I will present a few specific ideas we have found useful toward incorporating these skills into daily life.

Tool #1: Training Attention:

A few specific ideas that I have found useful, particularly when beginning to train attention are summarized below.

- Beginner's eyes – Look at an object (even a familiar object) with a completely open mind as if looking at it for the first time. Each object around you would thus be novel, unique and precious.
- Designer's eyes – Look at the object as if you personally designed it. The purpose is not to look with hypervigilant critical focus, but with appreciative admiring eyes.
- Meeting after a long time – Meet your loved ones as if you are meeting them after a long time. Thus, at the end of the day when you meet your spouse, instead of sharing just a "Hi" and then getting absorbed in your world, pull yourself out into their presence and make a purposeful effort to know how they are doing and what is new in their life. This will be much more enjoyable compared to playing the momentum of your work or activities in your mind. When listening to your loved ones, try not to multitask.
- Bless you – To the first 20 people you meet during the day, send a silent "bless you" from your eyes. You do not have to say anything; just convey this warm message from your eyes. See how you feel at the end of the morning.
- Call for help – When a loved one or colleague seems frustrated, upset or even angry, remember that in most situations it will not help to react adversely to it. It is best to remember that, *"An expression other than love is often a call for help."*

Tool #2: Interpretation –

A few specific themes that might be useful with respect to the concepts within interpretation are summarized below.

1. Gratitude –

Morning thought: I am grateful for whatever this day will bring, life's pleasures or life's lessons

Additional concepts related to gratitude:

* Gratitude as a first thought in the morning

  - Gratitude for the past, present and future
  - Gratitude for those who help me and those who seek my help
  - Gratitude for material, intangible, and spiritual
  - Gratitude for life's pleasures as well as life's lessons

* Gratitude during the day and as a last thought at the end of the day

  - Recognize and acknowledge kindness
  - Recognize life's blessings in the daily miracles
  - Recognize life's blessings in the daily challenges

Gratitude as a way of being: Grateful for the gift of the present moment; Gratitude as a background state

2. Compassion –

Morning thought: I will be compassionate toward everyone I meet today

Additional concepts related to compassion:

* Find connectedness with others
* Recognize the universality of pain, loss and suffering
* Practice compassion with nothing expected in return
* Avoid compassion fatigue (keep the perspective)
* Meditation on compassion

  - Include others in your circle
  - Find similarity with others
  - Intend to decrease pain and suffering

3. Acceptance –

Morning thought: Everyone I meet today I will accept them just as they are; I will accept myself today just as I am

Additional concepts related to acceptance:

* Develop Objectivity, Flexibility, Pursuit of Truth, and Willingness

* Understand universality of finiteness, suffering, change, and interconnectedness
* Live with confidence (faith) and optimism
* Understand circles of control, influence and lack of control
* One minute rule – if you have to criticize someone, limit that critique to one minute
* Understand link between acceptance and happiness
* Stop and smell the roses
* Accept others just as you wish to be accepted
* Know that a step back often is a move forward
* Know that some things you desire…some you are willing to accept
* Keep realistic expectations
* As long as you live, what is right about you trumps what is wrong about you
* Put greatest effort in what is important and controllable
* You may occasionally need an island of mindlessness

4. Meaning and Purpose –

Morning thought: I will focus today on the long-term meaning and purpose of my life

Additional concepts related to meaning and purpose:

* Understand the three key components of meaning:

   Relationships; Work; Spirituality

* Understand short-term vs. long-term meaning and the importance of aligning them
* Relationships – Understand your tribe; Positivity / Negativity ratio; Enhance your power to listen; Broaden zone of acceptance; Know that others could be right even if they think different
* Work – Balance work and leisure; Consider your work your calling; Become more comfortable with uncertainty
* Spirituality – Understand different definitions of spirituality; discover your own spirituality

5. Forgiveness –

Morning thought: I forgive for today anyone who might hurt my feelings; I forgive for today all my mistakes of the past, known and unknown

Additional concepts related to forgiveness:

* Understand what is forgiveness
   * It is not condoning, denying, justifying, excusing
   * It is a voluntary choice, for you, to live by your principles

* Understand reasons for forgiveness
  * Forgiveness improves several health outcomes
  * Forgiveness helps decrease anger
  * Forgiveness is a moral good
  * Forgiveness frees up the mind to focus on the future
  * Forgiveness improves relationships
  * We are forgiven, likely several times, every single day
  * Eventually all of us will have to forgive and / or forget
  * Every scripture we revere preaches the virtues of forgiveness
  * Most of the greatest persons we admire practiced (or practice) and taught (or teach) forgiveness
* Understand pearls related to forgiveness
  * Pearl #1. Consider forgiveness a lifelong process
  * Pearl #2. It is okay to be selfish in forgiveness (altruistic selfishness)
  * Pearl #3. Broaden your world view to include imperfections
  * Pearl #4. Try to understand others' actions
  * Pearl #5. Consider forgiveness as an opportunity
  * Pearl #6. Exercise the privilege to forgive as soon as you recognize the need for it
  * Pearl #7. Forgive gracefully without creating a burden on the forgiven
  * Pearl #8. Forgive before others seek your forgiveness
  * Pearl #9. Look forward to forgiving
  * Pearl #10. Extend your forgiveness toward what might even transpire in the future
  * Pearl #11. Praying for others increases your ability to forgive
  * Pearl #12. Prevent future situations where you may have a need to forgive
  * Pearl #13: Lower your expectations
  * Pearl #14: Have a low threshold to seek forgiveness
* Understand that we all desire to be forgiven
* Understand difference between willful and innocent mistakes
* Understand that the harm done to you may have helped you
* Understand the value of compassion and acceptance
* Practice forgiveness imagery if needed
* Develop pre-emptive forgiveness

An important final point: To incorporate these skills into your daily life, think of three things to do: Read (about these ideas); Discuss (these ideas with like minded people); and Practice (embody these ideas into your daily life). Knowledge, thereby becomes action and action becomes habit.

Appendix III: Daily Journal

I am including here the first seven pages of a daily diary we have developed for this program. Keeping a daily diary provides you the structure and also is a wonderful companion. I would highly recommend for you to make use of the daily diary, at least for the first twelve weeks of the practice.

Each page of the diary correlates with one day of practice. Described below are some instructions you might find useful with the diary. Please look over one page of the diary before you read the instructions further.

Tips for the Daily Diary:

Today's Theme – This field is prefilled based on the day. If you prefer another theme for the day, please replace what is prefilled with the new theme by just writing the new theme in the blank space.

Anchoring thought – The anchoring thought is related to the daily theme. I invite you to focus on the anchoring thought at least once during the morning, day time and at night.

Joyful Attention –

- Planned (set intention) – Plan the previous evening when and how many times will you practice joyful attention.
- Accomplished – Note at the end of the day when and how many times were you able to practice joyful attention.

Kind Attention –

- Planned (set intention) – Plan the previous evening approximately how many times will you practice kind attention. You do not have to be very precise here and could just say 10 or 20 times every day.
- Accomplished – Note at the end of the day approximately how many times you were able to practice kind attention.

Meditation –

- Planned (set intention) – Plan the previous evening approximately for how long will you practice meditation.
- Accomplished – Note at the end of the day approximately for how long were you able to practice meditation.

<u>Daily Journal</u> –

Write your thoughts and experiences in the first person in the journal.

If you wish to use this diary to help with your practice, please photocopy the following seven pages based on the number of weeks you plan on using the daily diary.

Name/ID

Date:	Day: Monday	Today's Theme: Gratitude	
Anchoring thought:	Morning: I am grateful for all this day will bring		☐
	Day: I am grateful for all this day is bringing		☐
	Night: I am grateful for all this day has brought		☐
Joyful Attention		Planned (Set intention)	Accomplished
	Morning		☐ ☐
	Day time		☐ ☐
	Evening		☐ ☐
	Night		☐ ☐
Kind Attention			
Meditation		minutes	minutes
Journal			

Name/ID

Date:	Day: Tuesday	Today's Theme: Compassion	
Anchoring thought:	Morning: I will be compassionate to everyone I meet today		☐
	Day: I am being compassionate to everyone I am meeting today		☐
	Night: I tried my best to be compassionate to everyone I met today		☐
Joyful Attention		Planned (Set intention)	Accomplished
	Morning		☐ ☐
	Day time		☐ ☐
	Evening		☐ ☐
	Night		☐ ☐
Kind Attention			
Meditation		_____ minutes	_____ minutes
Journal			

Name/ID

Date:	Day: Wednesday	Today's Theme: Acceptance	
Anchoring thought:	Morning: I will try my best to accept (others, myself, and my situation)		☐
	Day: I am trying my best to accept (others, myself, and my situation)		☐
	Night: I tried my best to accept (others, myself, and my situation)		☐
Joyful Attention		Planned (Set intention)	Accomplished
	Morning		☐ ☐
	Day time		☐ ☐
	Evening		☐ ☐
	Night		☐ ☐
Kind Attention			
Meditation		_____ minutes	_____ minutes
Journal			

Name/ID

Date:	Day: Thursday	Today's Theme: Meaning & Purpose	
Anchoring thought:	Morning: I will live my day with the higher meaning of my life		☐
	Day: I am living my day with the higher meaning of my life		☐
	Night: I tried my best to live my day with the higher meaning of my life		☐
Joyful Attention		Planned (Set intention)	Accomplished
	Morning		☐ ☐
	Day time		☐ ☐
	Evening		☐ ☐
	Night		☐ ☐
Kind Attention			
Meditation		_____ minutes	_____ minutes
Journal			

Name/ID

Date:	Day: Friday	Today's Theme: Forgiveness	
Anchoring thought:	Morning: I will try my best to forgive (others and myself)		☐
	Day: I am trying my best to forgive (others and myself)		☐
	Night: I tried my best to forgive (others and myself)		☐
Joyful Attention		Planned (Set intention)	Accomplished
	Morning		☐ ☐
	Day time		☐ ☐
	Evening		☐ ☐
	Night		☐ ☐
Kind Attention			
Meditation		_____ minutes	_____ minutes
Journal			

Name/ID _____

Date:	Day: Saturday	Today's Theme: Celebration	
Anchoring thought:	Morning: I will focus today on the little pleasures of daily life		☐
	Day: I am focusing today on the little pleasures of daily life		☐
	Night: I tried my best to focus today on the little pleasures of daily life		☐
Joyful Attention		Planned (Set intention)	Accomplished
	Morning		☐ ☐
	Day time		☐ ☐
	Evening		☐ ☐
	Night		☐ ☐
Kind Attention			
Meditation		_____ minutes	_____ minutes
Journal			

Name/ID

Date:	Day: Sunday	Today's Theme: Reflection/Prayer	
Anchoring thought:	Morning: I will reflect on the higher principles / spirituality		☐
	Day: I am reflecting on the higher principles / spirituality		☐
	Night: I reflected on the higher principles / spirituality		☐
Joyful Attention		Planned (Set intention)	Accomplished
	Morning		☐ ☐
	Day time		☐ ☐
	Evening		☐ ☐
	Night		☐ ☐
Kind Attention			
Meditation		_____ minutes	_____ minutes
Journal			

Appendix IV – The breath and the body

Breath offers an excellent tool for cultivating a deeper attention. A few reasons why breath offers an excellent tool to help train your attention include:

1) Breath is always available;
2) Breath is rhythmic and the rate can be changed at will, allowing an individual to join the breath at a personally chosen rate that feels comfortable;
3) Paying attention to the breath relaxes the mind;
4) Relaxed breath has several positive health-related effects;
5) Breath can be made increasingly subtle and your attempt to continue to appreciate its subtle state trains your senses;
6) Breath reflects the state of impermanence, one cycle merging into the next, just as life might be;
7) Breath does not have a form or structure. This lack of structure, while initially an impediment, is later helpful as it allows you to become comfortable with uncertainty;
8) You share the breath with others—what you exhale others inhale and *vice versa*. Breath, thus connects you with others in a tangible way. Most animals and plants breathe, and a focus on breath may remind you of your intimate connection with them. In fact, the whole world joins together in collective breathing at each moment.

The primary limitation with the breath is that in the initial stages you have to take extra time away from your busy day to practice breathing exercises. Further, with no previous attention training, focus on the breath can easily take you inward into the mind and back into the attention black holes. Thus, it might be optimal to use breath as an anchor only after your attention has somewhat stabilized and toned up using world as the initial focus.

There are many ways of attending to the breath. They start from simple breath awareness to deeper states of meditation. The simpler the technique, the greater is the likelihood that you will be able to do it for the long term. Throughout the program, try to practice diaphragmatic breathing. One good way to practice breathing exercises is to imagine filling a cup with water when you inhale. Just as the cup fills from the bottom up, you fill your lower lungs and then the upper lungs by expanding your belly and moving your diaphragm. You could even gently keep your hands on the belly and pay attention to their movement during inhalation. During exhalation, just as the cup empties from top below, empty the upper lungs first and then the lower lungs. If any of this seems confusing, just take deep and slow breaths in a way that feels comfortable to you.

The first exercise I share will guide you to observe your breath at a static point, the tip of your nose. In this exercise practice your skills to be an impartial witness.

Exercise 1. Breath awareness 1

1. *Sit in a comfortable, dimly lit, quiet, and safe place with your eyes closed. You can choose any posture you like other than lying down on the bed (you might go off to sleep). Also avoid doing this exercise immediately post meal.*

2. *Spend the first two minutes paying attention to all the sounds you hear in the environment. Allow your awareness to travel to the source of the sounds. Try to avoid making any judgments about the sounds.*

3. *At this point, gradually settle your awareness and bring it to your breath.*

4. *Practice deep, slow, diaphragmatic breathing for the duration of the exercise.*

5. *Adapt a breathing rate and depth that feels comfortable.*

6. *Visualize your breath at the tip of your nostril. Feel the subtle, cool breath as it flows in and a warm, cozy breath as you breathe out.*

7. *Keep your attention at the tip of the nostril for the next few minutes watching the inward and outward flowing breath.*

8. *Now allow your breath to become subtle until you reach a point when you just about stop feeling the flow.*

9. *Keep your awareness rested on the tip of the nostril with this subtle breath for the next few minutes.*

10. *Continue this exercise for as long as you like, at least for ten minutes.*

In the next exercise we will track the movement of the breath.

Exercise 2. Breath awareness 2

1. *Sit in a comfortable, dimly lit, quiet, and safe place with your eyes closed. You can choose any posture you like, other than lying down on the bed (you might go off to sleep). Also avoid doing this exercise immediately post meal.*

2. *Spend the first two minutes paying attention to all the sounds you hear in the environment. Allow your awareness to travel to the source of the sounds. Try to avoid making any judgments about the sounds.*

3. *At this point, gradually settle your awareness and bring it to your breath.*

4. *Practice deep, slow, diaphragmatic breathing for the duration of the exercise.*

5. *Adapt a breathing rate and depth that feels comfortable.*

6. *Visualize your inhaled breath traveling from the tip of your nostril to the farthest reaches of your brain (upper body).*

7. *Now, visualize your exhaled breath traveling from your brain out to the tip of the nose.*

8. *Visualize your inhaled breath traveling from the tip of your nostril to the farthest reaches of your legs (lower body).*

9. *Now, visualize your exhaled breath traveling from your legs out to the tip of the nose.*

10. *Repeat this exercise for as long as you like, at least for ten minutes.*

There are many variants possible to the breathing exercises and you are welcome to change and adapt them the way you like. It might help to work with a well-trained yoga teacher if you wish to learn the more advanced techniques. One simple variation is to pay attention to the movements of the abdominal wall instead of the tip of the nose. Another common approach is to pay attention to the pause between the inhalation and exhalation.

The next exercise I wish you to learn is to focus on body awareness. Your body offers an excellent focus for attention that is always available and enjoys the relaxation that comes with paying attention.

Exercise 3. Body awareness in six breaths

1. *Sit in a comfortable, dimly lit, quiet, and safe place with your eyes closed. You can choose any posture you like, other than lying down on the bed (you might go off to sleep). Also avoid doing this exercise immediately post meal.*

2. *Spend the first two minutes paying attention to all the sounds you hear in the environment. Allow your awareness to travel to the source of the sounds. Try to avoid making any judgments about the sounds.*

3. *At this point, gradually settle your awareness and bring it to your breath.*

4. *Practice deep, slow, diaphragmatic breathing for the duration of the exercise.*

5. *Adapt a breathing rate and depth that feels comfortable.*

6. *Take a deep breath as you bring your awareness to your head. Imagine your brain filling up with soothing white light. Gradually exhale this breath.*

7. *Take a deep breath as you bring your awareness to your face and neck. Imagine your face and neck filling up with soothing white light. Gradually exhale this breath.*

8. *Take a deep breath as you bring your awareness to your chest. Imagine your chest filling up with soothing white light. Gradually exhale this breath.*

9. *Take a deep breath as you bring your awareness to your belly. Imagine your belly filling up with soothing white light. Gradually exhale this breath.*

10. *Take a deep breath as you bring your awareness to your arms and legs. Imagine your arms and legs filling up with soothing white light. Gradually exhale this breath.*

11. *Take a deep breath as you bring your awareness to your entire body. Imagine your entire body filling up with soothing white light. Gradually exhale this breath.*

12. *Continue this exercise for as long as you like and feel comfortable. Preferred duration is ten sets, which will take about ten minutes.*

A common variation of this exercise is to focus only on the body part rather than including body and breath. I prefer to combine the two; it helps to keep the deep breathing exercise as a background for most relaxation practices.

There are countless variations to breath and body exercises. The key is to keep the exercises simple, do enough repetitions, and persevere with the practice. Pick only a few exercises for daily practice so your time commitment is realistic. As you learn and experience these exercises, keep the clarity of your primary goal. It is to cultivate a deeper attention. With this attention extraneous thoughts will automatically settle. As you progress along this path, you will become your own teacher and find newer ways to develop your attention.

Acknowledgments

I am thankful to my family for all their understanding, support, and love. My wife Richa and daughter Gauri spent many months playing together as I worked in the quiet of our basement. The cushion of understanding and love they have provided has allowed me to bring this work to completion. My parents introduced me to meditation and have been wonderful role models.

I am grateful to my colleagues at Mayo Clinic Rochester for their support and inspiration. I am appreciative of Carla Paonessa and Debbie Fuehrer for their critical review of the manuscript.

In this effort, I stand on the shoulders of thousands of researchers and authors who have developed a large body of work that contributes toward this book. I hold them in the highest esteem and am indebted for their contributions.

Most of all, I am thankful to the true embodiments of divine I have been blessed to serve over the last two decades—my patients. I have truly gained more from them than I could ever share.

Peace be on earth and may it come through you.

Amit Sood, MD MSc

January 2011

About the Author

Dr. Amit Sood is the Director of Research and Practice in the Mayo Complementary and Integrative Medicine Program at Mayo Clinic. An Associate Professor of Medicine, he chairs the Mind Body Medicine Initiative. He completed his residency in Internal medicine at the Albert Einstein School of Medicine, earned an Integrative Medicine Fellowship from the University of Arizona, and a Masters in Clinical Research from Mayo Clinic College of Medicine. He has received several NIH and foundation grants for conducting research to develop and incorporate integrative and mind-body approaches into conventional medical care and to promote well being. He provides integrative and mind-body medicine consults to patients at the Mayo Complementary and Integrative Medicine Program in Rochester, MN.